Dear Reader,

My first book for Silhouette was released in August of 1991. Seeing *Patchwork Family* on the shelves was one of the biggest thrills of my life. This month, I'm celebrating another thrill…the publication of my fiftieth *and* fifty-first book in the same month.

What if I'm Pregnant…? and *If the Stick Turns Pink…* are stories about…you guessed it—the possibility of pregnancy for two very special couples. I hope these books represent what you've come to expect from my writing…heartwarming stories about good people finding love.

I'd like to take this opportunity to thank my readers. Without you I would have no voice, and I hope that you will continue to enjoy the stories I tell. I'd also like to take a moment to thank Silhouette and the many wonderful editors I've worked with over the years. Thank you for allowing me the honor of writing for you. It has truly been a pleasure.

Best,

Carla Cassidy

Dear Reader,

In the spirit of Valentine's Day, we have some wonderful stories for you this February from Silhouette Romance to guarantee that every day is filled with love and tenderness.

DeAnna Talcott puts a fresh spin on the tale of Cupid, who finally meets her match in *Cupid Jones Gets Married* (#1646), the latest in the popular SOULMATES series. And Carla Cassidy has been working overtime with her incredibly innovative, incredibly fun duo, *What if I'm Pregnant...?* (#1644) and *If the Stick Turns Pink...* (#1645), about the promise of love a baby could bring to two special couples!

Then Elizabeth Harbison takes us on a fairy-tale adventure in *Princess Takes a Holiday* (#1643). A glamour-weary royal who hides her identity meets the man of her dreams when her car breaks down in a small North Carolina town. In *Dude Ranch Bride* (#1642), Madeline Baker brings us strong, sexy Lakota Ethan Stormwalker, whose ex-flame shows up at his ranch in a wedding gown—without a groom! And in Donna Clayton's *Thunder in the Night* (#1647), the third in THE THUNDER CLAN family saga, a single act of kindness changes Conner Thunder's life forever....

Be sure to come back next month for more emotion-filled love stories from Silhouette Romance. Happy reading!

Mary-Theresa Hussey

Mary-Theresa Hussey
Senior Editor

Please address questions and book requests to:
Silhouette Reader Service
U.S.: 3010 Walden Ave., P.O. Box 1325, Buffalo, NY 14269
Canadian: P.O. Box 609, Fort Erie, Ont. L2A 5X3

What if I'm Pregnant...?

CARLA CASSIDY

50th
Book

SILHOUETTE *Romance*®
Published by Silhouette Books
America's Publisher of Contemporary Romance

To Frankie, Jr., the son of my heart.

Thank you for the joy you bring to my life.

SILHOUETTE BOOKS

ISBN 0-373-19644-X

WHAT IF I'M PREGNANT...?

Copyright © 2003 by Carla Bracale

This edition published by arrangement with Harlequin Books S.A.

® and TM are trademarks of Harlequin Books S.A., used under license.
Trademarks indicated with ® are registered in the United States Patent
and Trademark Office, the Canadian Trade Marks Office and in other
countries.

Visit Silhouette at www.eHarlequin.com

Printed in U.S.A.

Books by Carla Cassidy

CARLA CASSIDY

is an award-winning author who has written over fifty books for Silhouette. In 1995, she won Best Silhouette Romance from *Romantic Times* for *Anything for Danny*. In 1998, she also won a Career Achievement Award for Best Innovative Series from *Romantic Times*.

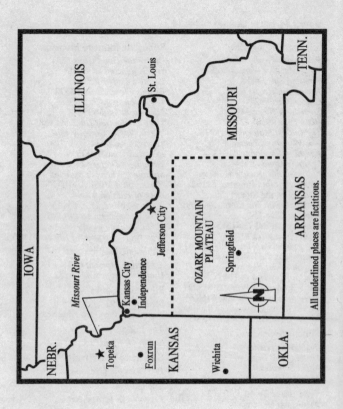

IOWA

NEBR.

ILLINOIS

St. Louis

MISSOURI

TENN.

Missouri River

Jefferson City

Kansas City
Independence

OZARK MOUNTAIN
PLATEAU

Springfield

ARKANSAS

Topeka

Foxrun

KANSAS

Wichita

N

OKLA.

All underlined places are fictitious.

Prologue

Colette Carson stood in her bathroom and pulled the pregnancy test out of the plastic shopping bag. Her fingers trembled as she opened the box and pulled out the test instrument and the directions.

She read the directions quickly, then looked at her reflection in the mirror over the sink. Her eyes were slightly swollen from her morning of tears, and her pale face radiated the torment of heartbreak that ached inside her.

She couldn't think about that, she thought as she scanned the directions to the test one last time. She absolutely, positively couldn't think about *him.*

Four weeks ago the only wish in her life had been to be pregnant, and she'd opted to become a single parent. She'd found a clinic that offered artificial insemination and had gone through the procedure.

Four weeks ago, all she'd wanted was to be pregnant, but that had been before she'd met *him,* before she'd fallen in love with *him* and had her heart broken into a million little pieces.

She stared down at the directions one last time. She'd bought the one she'd thought would be easiest to read. Within three minutes either a plus or minus sign would appear in the test window. Plus meant pregnant. Minus meant not pregnant.

Simple. Easy. Except that since she had been artificially inseminated her life had suddenly become complicated and she wasn't sure now if she wanted to be pregnant.

Deciding she could put it off no longer, she took the test, then set it on the counter and prepared to wait the three minutes.

"Oh, my," she muttered to herself. "What if I'm pregnant?"

Chapter One

Fourteen days.

Colette Carson entered her apartment, kicked off her shoes and dropped tiredly on the overstuffed beige sofa. It had been exactly fourteen days since she had been artificially inseminated and on every one of those days she'd wondered if her wish, her dream was about to come true.

If the procedure had been successful, then she would not only be the owner of Little Bit Baby Boutique, but she would become one of her own best customers. She smiled with sweet anticipation and touched her tummy lovingly.

She'd never been more ready for a baby than she was at this moment in her life. She was twenty-eight years old, her boutique was successful beyond her dreams and she was confident she could successfully raise a child alone.

She had approached the decision to become a mother as she had everything else in her life, with unemotional logic and careful clearheaded planning.

Looking at her watch, she realized Gina would be home at any minute and it was Colette's turn to cook dinner. She pulled herself up and off the sofa, thinking of the young woman who not only worked for her in her shop but had also become her roommate three weeks ago.

Gina Rothman was a sweet, considerate twenty-one-year-old, who was renting Colette's second bedroom until she could afford a place of her own.

An old friend had asked Colette if she could take in the young woman and Colette's initial response had been "no way."

After a string of bad roommates, Colette had decided she wasn't willing to share her living space ever again. She didn't need the rent money a roommate would bring in, and she certainly didn't need the headaches.

She was still trying to get over the horror of her last roommate, a woman named Trina who had been into primal screaming and practiced her yoga buck naked in Colette's living room.

But Margaret Jamison had begged, telling her that Gina Rothman was a sweet young woman eager to work hard and forge a path in the world for herself.

Finally Colette had relented. So far the arrangement had worked out remarkably well.

Gina appeared to have no hidden vices and seemed eager to learn everything Colette could teach her about running a business and living in the city.

In the kitchen Colette went to the refrigerator and peered in at the contents. There was a pound of hamburger, and she tried to decide whether she wanted to make a quick spaghetti sauce or tacos.

Before she could make up her mind, she heard the front door open, then slam shut. She left the kitchen and walked into the living room to see Gina putting the chain lock on the door.

"Spaghetti or tacos?" she asked her pretty young roommate.

Gina whirled around to face Colette, her big blue eyes widened in panic. "You've got to hide me," she exclaimed. She raced over to Colette and grabbed her hand. "You've got to tell him I don't live here, that you don't know who I am or where I live." The words spilled out of her as she shot a backward glance to the front door.

"Slow down," Colette replied with alarm. "What's going on? Who are you hiding from?" Great. She knew Gina was too good to be true. Had Gina neglected to mention a crazed stalker ex-boyfriend?

"Tanner. He's found me," Gina cried, tears springing to her eyes.

"Who is Tanner?" Colette asked, worry sweeping through her as she saw Gina's obvious anguish.

"My brother." The tears oozed from her eyes and ran in twin rivulets down her cheeks. "I know why he's here. He's come to take me back to that stupid ranch. He's so mean and hateful and he's never going to let me grow up, never!"

Colette relaxed somewhat with the information that apparently the threat was from a brother, not a nutty stalker. "All you need to do is explain to him that you're doing fine and don't want to go back to the ranch," she said gently.

Gina shook her head vehemently, her dark hair flying around her heart-shaped face. "You don't understand about Tanner. He won't listen to me...he never listens to me and Tanner always gets what he wants." She released her hold on Colette's hand and ran into her bedroom and slammed the door.

In the next instant a firm knock fell on the front door. Colette hesitated before answering, trying to assimilate what Gina had just told her. When Colette had taken Gina in, she'd known that this was Gina's first foray into the world.

Gina had left her family home in western Kansas and had moved here to Kansas City to begin an independent life. So, big brother has come to the big city to check up on her, Colette thought.

All she had to do was assure big brother, Tanner Rothman, that Gina wasn't being corrupted and was handling her new independence with maturity and good sense.

She unlocked her front door and pulled it open. All rational thought momentarily fled her brain as she eyed the tall, broad-shouldered cowboy with smoldering midnight-blue eyes.

He was clad in a pair of tight, faded jeans, a blue chambray shirt and boots. His hair was the same rich dark color as Gina's, cut short and emphasizing bold, strong features. Gina hadn't mentioned that her brother was a top quality hunk.

"Good evening," he said, his voice low and pleasant. "My name is Tanner Rothman and I'm here to speak with my sister."

He smiled, the pleasant gesture allowing Colette to relax somewhat. Gina had made him sound like a real ogre, but he appeared respectful and looked like a reasonable man—an incredibly handsome, reasonable man.

"Hi, I'm Colette Carson, Gina's roommate. Please, come in." She opened the door wider to allow him entry.

As he swept past her and into the living room, she caught his scent, a masculine fresh smell that was instantly pleasing.

"Please, have a seat." She gestured toward the sofa.

"No, thanks," he replied. "If I could just speak with Gina…" His dark blue eyes swept over her, then perused the surroundings, and Colette wondered if he was looking for something criminal or sinful, some ammunition he could use to get his sister to leave with him.

As Colette went to get Gina, she smiled to herself. He would be hard-pressed to find anything to use against Gina. The apartment was a reflection of Colette's life—well organized, efficient and clean.

"Gina." She knocked on the young woman's bedroom door.

Gina cracked open the door and peered out at Colette. "Is he gone?" she asked.

"No, but he says he just wants to talk to you," Colette replied.

"I don't want to talk to him," Gina exclaimed, keeping her voice low. "He'll talk me into doing something I don't want to do. He'll win...he always wins."

"Gina, how are you going to convince him that you're ready to be out on your own if you hide in your bedroom like a child?"

Gina's pretty features transformed into a thoughtful frown. "Okay," she relented. "I'll come out and talk to him, but only if you stay with me."

It was Colette's turn to frown. "I don't think I should get involved in—"

"Please," Gina begged. "You don't have to say anything or do anything. Just sit next to me, and that will give me the strength not to let him talk me into anything I'll regret later.''

''All right,'' Colette relented.

Together the two women went back into the living room where Tanner Rothman stood at the eighth-floor window that offered a view of the skyscraper next door.

He turned as they entered the room, and again Colette was struck by how utterly handsome he was. His sensual lips curved up into another smile as he eyed his sister with obvious fondness. ''Hello, Gina.''

Gina sank down on the sofa, and Colette sat next to her. ''How did you find me, Tanner?'' she asked.

''That's not important right now,'' he replied smoothly. ''How are you? It's been three weeks and you haven't called or written or anything.''

Gina gazed at the wall to the left of Tanner. ''I've been busy,'' she replied.

''And I've been worried,'' Tanner replied.

Colette wished she were anywhere but here. She felt like a fly on the wall who needed to fly into another room and leave these two people some privacy.

Gina flushed. ''There's nothing to worry about. As you can see I'm doing just fine.''

''I was wondering if I could take you out to dinner this evening.''

''I'm not hungry,'' Gina replied with a touch of defiance.

Colette watched the brother and sister. The tension in the air was thick and palpable.

"It's almost seven and I know you just got off work," Tanner continued. "You have to be hungry. Come on, Gina, all I'm asking for is to take you out for a nice dinner." His voice held a soft appeal.

Gina hesitated, her gaze going to Colette, who carefully kept her features schooled in total neutrality. Gina looked back at her brother. "Okay, I'll have dinner with you, but only if Colette comes with us."

Colette gasped in surprise. "Oh, I don't think—"

"Fine," Tanner replied, overriding the objection Colette was about to make. He moved away from the window and walked back to the front door.

"I saw what looked like a nice barbecue place on the next block while I was walking here. Why don't we meet there in half an hour or so. That will give you ladies time to freshen up or whatever."

Although Colette wanted to vehemently protest any arrangement that included her, before she had an opportunity Tanner was gone, leaving only a trace of his masculine cologne lingering in the air.

"Gina, I really think you and your brother should talk to each other without me," Colette said. "I'll just make myself a salad here. You meet him."

"Colette, please come with me," Gina replied, her big blue eyes begging with appeal.

"You're of legal age, Gina. He can't drag you back

with him kicking and screaming," Colette protested. "You don't need me there."

"If you don't go, then I won't go, and then he'll just come back here. Please."

Colette looked at her young roommate and was unable to tell her no. She knew what it was like to have a dream and be surrounded by people who didn't think you were capable of achieving anything.

"All right, dinner tonight," she relented. "But then you're on your own where your brother is concerned."

"Thank you," Gina said with obvious relief.

"I'm going to change my clothes," Colette said, wanting to get into something a little more casual than the power suit she'd worn to work.

As she went into her bedroom, she vowed to herself that she would eat dinner and keep her mouth shut. There was no way she intended to get into a battle between the handsome cowboy and his baby sister.

Tanner sat in the restaurant waiting for his sister and her roommate to arrive. He was irritated that Gina had invited Colette Carson to join them. From all the information he'd gathered about the pretty blonde, he had a feeling she was exactly the wrong kind of influence for his sweet, innocent sister.

Still, he'd been shocked by the instantaneous attraction he'd felt when Colette had opened her door to him and he'd had his first glimpse of her.

Her blond hair had been a short, curly halo, a perfect foil for her delicate features and whiskey-colored eyes. Clad in a two-piece navy suit, she'd looked like the cool, driven professional his sources had told him she was.

He'd wanted to get Gina alone, knew that if he had some time with her he'd be able to convince her that what she'd done by leaving school and moving to Kansas City was not in her best interest. But now it seemed he wouldn't have time with Gina alone...at least not tonight.

"Would you like a drink while you wait for your party?" The waitress gave him a flirtatious smile.

Tanner would have loved a Scotch on the rocks, but knew he needed to be clearheaded for the confrontation to come. "A glass of iced tea will be just fine," he said.

As the waitress left his table, he once again thought of his sister. He didn't understand Gina at all, suspected that this impromptu move to the city was a belated surge of rebellion.

He'd given her three weeks to come to her senses, but that hadn't happened. Now he needed to deal with the situation quickly and efficiently. And that's exactly what he intended to do.

He rose as he saw the object of his thoughts and her roommate entering the restaurant. He motioned them over to the secluded table, noting that Colette had changed from her business suit into a pair of slim-legged dark brown slacks and a dark-brown-and-beige tunic top. She looked casual, yet coolly elegant.

A warning buzzer went off in his head as he realized his sister was wearing a very similar outfit. "Good evening." He greeted them with a smile.

Colette returned his smile. Gina didn't. She pulled out the chair opposite Tanner, leaving Colette to sit at his side. As Colette slid into a chair at his left, Tanner caught a whiff of her scent, a rich floral fragrance that instantly reminded him of the best of spring on his ranch.

"I hope you like barbecue," he said to Colette. "I know it's one of Gina's favorites."

"Not anymore," Gina replied petulantly.

Gina's childish behavior only confirmed Tanner's belief that she wasn't ready for the giant leap she'd made from the ranch to independence and city life.

"Barbecue is fine," Colette said smoothly and picked up the menu from in front of her. Gina did the same, holding the menu up high so Tanner couldn't see her face.

Tanner smiled inwardly. He knew his sister very well. She was angry and defensive, and that usually meant she knew she was wrong. It shouldn't be a problem convincing her to return to the ranch with him.

At that moment the waitress appeared at their table and took their orders. Once she departed, Tanner eyed his sister once again. "Bugsy had puppies a week ago,'' he said, then turned to Colette. ''Bugsy is Gina's golden retriever.''

For a moment Gina's petulance fell away and her eyes sparkled as she leaned forward. ''Oh, how many?''

''Four, two males and two females,'' he replied.

''And Bugsy is okay?''

''Came through like the champ she is.'' He paused a beat. ''She misses you.''

''Don't even go there,'' Gina replied and leaned back in her chair, crossing her arms in a gesture of defensiveness.

''Gina, I was just stating a fact. I wasn't trying to manipulate your emotions,'' he replied.

He suddenly realized he was going to have to be a lot more subtle than he'd thought. Perhaps what he needed was the aid of somebody else in this...and that somebody else was sitting at his left. Gina might not listen to him, but he had a feeling she would listen to the lovely Colette.

He turned and looked at her, wondering if he could charm her to his side of this issue. She was obviously uncomfortable and would have preferred not being here. Her fingers toyed with the cloth napkin in her lap and she appeared to find a nearby potted plant utterly fascinating.

''Miss Carson, I understand you own a store that sells baby things,'' he said.

She smiled and he couldn't help but notice that she

had pretty cupid lips, lips that appeared just perfect for kissing. "Yes, the Little Bit Baby Boutique. I officially opened the doors two years ago."

Their conversation halted as the waitress appeared with their food. She served them, chatting about the weather and how busy the restaurant had been since the coming of spring, then departed.

"I would assume owning your own business requires a lot of time and energy," Tanner said as he cut into his thick T-bone steak.

"It does," Colette agreed. "Which is why I was so pleased to hire Gina. She's been a real godsend and is a wonderful salesclerk." She smiled in obvious affection at Gina, who smiled back with the shine of hero worship in her eyes.

"Gina's very bright," Tanner replied. Far too bright to work for minimum wage as a clerk in a baby store, he thought.

His biggest fear was that not only would Gina not live up to her intellectual potential, but that a smooth-talking city slicker would take advantage of her, break her heart and leave her not only working in a store for babies, but shopping there, as well. Then she would never fulfill the future Tanner had envisioned for her. All his hard work on her behalf would be for naught.

"Gina tells me you run a big ranch in Kansas, so you must know about long hours and expended energy," Colette said.

Tanner nodded. "Yes, it definitely requires hard work and long hours...especially this time of year."

"Then I'm sure you're eager to get back," Gina quipped.

Tanner laughed at her lack of subtlety. "You know me, Gina. Family has always been more important than anything else in the world." Again he turned to Colette. "You have family, Miss Carson?"

"Please, call me Colette," she replied. "And my family consists of just my mother and me."

"She lives here in town?"

"Yes, but unfortunately we aren't very close." She turned her attention to Gina. "The salad is wonderful, isn't it."

Tanner frowned and cut off another bite of his steak. She wasn't close to her mother. As far as Tanner was concerned, that was just another reason to get Gina away from her influence.

Tanner knew the importance of family. Colette Carson had no idea how lucky she was to have a mother. But Tanner knew all about being without a mother and a father and the importance of hanging on to the family left behind. And his family was Gina.

"So, what kind of a ranch do you have, Mr. Rothman?" Colette asked.

He grinned. "Make it Tanner, and we raise cattle. I've got a large herd of Charolais and a large herd of Hereford cows."

"Oh, is one for milk and one for meat?" she asked.

Both Tanner and Gina laughed. "They're both meat cows," Gina replied.

"Don't be embarrassed," Tanner said to Colette, whose cheeks had turned a charming pink. "I wouldn't know a bunting from a bonnet when it comes to babies."

She laughed, the sound musical and sweet. "I'm afraid I don't know much about cows."

"Tanner also breeds horses," Gina explained. "Two Hearts has been responsible for several championship quarter horses."

"Two Hearts...that's the name of your ranch?" Colette asked.

"Yeah. Gina named the place," Tanner explained, remembering the day the ranch had been named. It had been two days after their parents' funerals as they had stood on the front porch and gazed out across the expanse of pasture and fields that surrounded the ranch house.

"Tanner didn't like it," Gina replied. "He thought it sounded too feminine." She gazed at Tanner and smiled. "But he said if Two Hearts is what I wanted, then that's what it would be."

"I always did spoil you," Tanner exclaimed.

They finished the meal talking about less personal things—the beautiful spring weather, the latest movies they'd seen and the most recent political scandal.

Tanner found his gaze drawn again and again to

Colette, slightly irritated by the fact that he found her so attractive.

When she smiled a dimple danced in one of her cheeks, and when she grew thoughtful she pursed her lips in what appeared to be a direct invitation to explore their creamy texture.

She seemed to be as bright as she was pretty and their conversation was lively and surprisingly stimulating. But he wasn't here to enjoy the company of Gina's roommate and boss. He reminded himself of this as the meal came to an end and they each ordered a cup of coffee.

Tanner wrapped his hands around the thick mug of coffee and decided it was time to renew his campaign to get Gina back on the ranch where she belonged.

"Gina. I'm worried about you," he said, deciding that authoritative demands wouldn't work. He needed to appeal to her on another level.

"There's nothing to worry about," she protested. "I'm doing just fine."

"You don't understand the dangers of city life," he continued. "You've been sheltered all your life. You aren't ready for this, Gina." He reached across the table and took one of her hands in his. "You know I wouldn't be here if I wasn't worried sick about you."

Gina pulled her hand away, a pained expression on her pretty features. She looked at Colette, as if seeking some sort of support.

"She seems to be handling her new independence quite well," Colette said. "I was on my own at her age and I've managed to do pretty well for myself."

Tanner forced a smile, hoping it hid his irritation. "But Gina isn't you. Besides, I couldn't help but notice that your apartment isn't in the best area of town and there is no security to speak of."

Although Tanner hoped he'd managed to hide his own irritation, he saw the spark of the same emotion that lit Colette's eyes. "This area is in the process of rejuvenation. It was a good business decision on my part to put my shop here and live in the same area."

"That's fine for you, but it isn't fine for Gina," he replied. "She simply isn't ready for this jump into city life and being on her own. She's too young, and ill equipped to handle life on her own."

"If you're so concerned about Gina's life here, why don't you stick around for a few days, watch her working, see how well she's handling things?" Colette suggested.

Gina looked horrified at the very idea. Tanner frowned. Hanging out for a few days in Kansas City was not in his plans, but then he hadn't expected Gina to have such a strong support system in her roommate.

"That's a great idea," he replied, hoping neither of the women saw the intense frustration building inside him. This wasn't working out as he'd planned and Tanner didn't like being thwarted.

"Tanner, I know how busy the spring season is at the ranch," Gina exclaimed, horror still radiating from her eyes. "I'm sure you can't spare any time to just hang out here with me and Colette."

"On the contrary, Gina, I've always told you where my priorities lie, and family has always been my number one priority," he replied. He paused a moment and took a sip of his coffee, then continued. "Besides, I've got good men working for me back at the ranch. They'll keep things running smoothly while I'm gone. I've already checked into the hotel down the street, and maybe spending a couple of days hanging out will reassure me."

He forced a smile. He had no intention of being reassured. He did not intend to leave Kansas City without Gina in tow. Legally he had no leverage. She was of age and could refuse to return to the ranch where she belonged.

But Tanner knew there was more than one way to skin a cat, and he knew the best way to get Gina back where she belonged was to gain Colette's support.

He gazed at the lovely blonde, a rush of adrenaline sweeping through him as he realized that was one cat he wouldn't mind skinning at all.

Chapter Two

"I can't believe you did that," Gina exclaimed the moment the two women were once again alone in the apartment.

"Did what?" Colette asked as she kicked off her shoes and flopped down on the sofa.

"Suggested that Tanner stick around for a few days." She paced back and forth in front of Colette, her slender body stiff with tension. "That just gives him more opportunity to manipulate me into doing what he wants, not what I want." Gina sat in the chair opposite the sofa.

"Gina, I think he's just worried about you, and after a day or two of seeing you here, I'm sure he'll realize you're doing just fine."

Gina leaned forward. "You don't know him, Colette. He's relentless. Don't be fooled by his charm, don't be fooled by him. He's so cursedly stubborn, he doesn't even have a girlfriend.''

Colette held up her hands in a gesture of helplessness. ''Gina, this is between you and your brother. He doesn't have to try to charm me. It's you he wants to take back to the family ranch.''

''He wants me to go to school and get a job teaching in the local grade school and eventually marry Walt Tibberman.''

''Who is Walt Tibberman?'' Colette asked curiously.

Gina stopped her pacing and sat in the chair opposite Colette. ''Walt works on the ranch for Tanner. He's a nice guy and a hard worker and I know he has a thing for me, but I don't feel any sparks with him. There's no magic between us.''

Colette bit her tongue. She didn't believe in that kind of magic. As far as she was concerned, love was a nice illusion used to sell greeting cards and flowers, a nice word to justify lust and passion. As far as Colette was concerned, love was for needy, clingy women who were afraid to live their lives alone.

She stood and smiled at her young roommate. ''Gina, if this is what you want, to stay and build a life here, then stand strong against your brother. And with that bit of advice, I'm going to bed.''

A few minutes later as Colette changed out of her clothes and into the short cotton nightshirt she always wore to bed, she couldn't help but think about Tanner Rothman.

She had not only found him ruggedly handsome to look at, but utterly charming, as well. His obvious concern for his sister, his desire to make certain she was okay, only added to his attractiveness.

A slight wistfulness filled her as she slid beneath the sheet and into bed. She wished there had been somebody who had been concerned about her when she'd been eighteen years old and had struck out on her own.

Gina might see her big brother as a pain in her backside, but she had no idea how lucky she was to have somebody who cared about her and her well-being.

Colette shoved these thoughts aside. She rarely thought about what she'd never had, instead focused her thoughts and energy on attaining what she wanted. She'd learned at a very early age that she could depend on nobody but herself.

She placed a hand on her tummy, wondering if even now, at this very moment, a little soul was inside her. How she hoped, how she prayed that the artificial insemination had been successful. This child of hers would have all the love, all the care, all the dreams that nobody had ever taken the time to give to Colette.

She frowned sleepily. Funny, she wondered where Tanner and Gina's parents were in all this. Neither of them had mentioned what their parents wanted. In fact, in the weeks that Gina and Colette had worked together, lived together, she hadn't mentioned any mother or father.

It wasn't her business, she told herself firmly. Just as Gina's life wasn't her business. And no matter how handsome, no matter how charming Tanner Rothman was, within days he'd be back at his ranch living his own life and she would continue hers...hopefully anticipating the birth of the child who would fill her world with love.

With this pleasant thought in mind, Colette fell asleep.

It was just after eight the next morning when she left the apartment to walk the three blocks to her shop. It was a gorgeous spring day. The sun was already up, shining down warmth on her shoulders, and the scent of sweet flowers rode the air from a nearby truck stand that sold fruits, vegetables and flowers.

Although the shop didn't officially open until nine-thirty, Colette liked to get there early in the mornings. She always stopped into the local café for fresh bagels, then went on to The Little Bit Baby Boutique and made a pot of coffee.

She enjoyed the quiet time before customers began to arrive, and often the bagel breakfast was all that sustained her through the day. Usually the store was too busy for her to take any kind of a lunch break.

As usual, the café was busy with clerks and office workers whose businesses were located in the downtown area. Colette went directly to the counter, where "to go" orders were placed.

"Hi, Johnny," she said, greeting the heavyset older man behind the counter.

"Hey, doll." He grinned at her. "The usual?"

She nodded, then remembered that it was possible Tanner would spend part of his day at the shop. "Why don't you double it."

Johnny raised a grizzled gray eyebrow as he placed the fresh bagels into a paper sack. "What did you do? Skip dinner last night?"

She laughed. "You know me, Johnny, I rarely miss a meal."

"Here you go, doll. Take it easy."

She took the bag of bagels he handed her, then paid him his amount due. "Stay out of trouble, Johnny," she said.

"That's one thing an ex-con always tries to do," he replied with a teasing grin.

She smiled and whirled around to leave and ran smack dab into Tanner Rothman's broad chest. He grabbed her by the shoulders to steady her and grinned down at her. "Good morning," he said.

"Good morning," she replied, and quickly stepped back from him, far too aware of the clean, masculine scent of him and the hard muscle of the chest she'd just made contact with.

"Headed to the store?" he asked.

She nodded. "I always stop here for Johnny's

freshly baked bagels before going in. I bought extra this morning if you'd like to have one."

"Sounds good. I was wondering what time you all normally got to the store."

"I usually get there by eight-thirty or so. Gina doesn't come in until noon," she explained.

They left the café and started walking down the sidewalk toward the baby boutique. She tried not to notice how utterly devastating he looked in his tight, worn blue jeans and a short-sleeved dark blue T-shirt that exposed powerful forearms and deepened the hue of his eyes.

However, it was difficult not to be aware of Tanner's potent sexuality and handsomeness when they passed several women on the street and they openly stared at him with admiring eyes.

"The guy who runs the café is an ex-con?" he asked.

Instantly Colette knew he was thinking all kinds of horrors about a dangerous criminal in the neighborhood and his innocent little sister. "Thirty years ago Johnny robbed a couple of houses. He got caught, served eighteen months and apparently came out of prison a changed man. Besides running his café, he's now a member of the chamber of commerce and is involved in several community groups working to prevent crime."

She stopped at the door to her shop and withdrew a set of keys from her purse. She unlocked the door then turned to face him with a teasing smile. "You can't use ex-con Johnny as a reason for Gina to go home."

One corner of his mouth turned upward in a sexy smile that caused heat to flood through Colette. "Am I that transparent?" he asked.

"In this particular instance you were," she replied and turned to open the door, needing something else to focus on besides the inviting heat his smile had evoked in her.

"Welcome to the Little Bit Baby Boutique," she said as she flipped on the overhead lights, then relocked the door as he stepped in behind her. "If you want to come on back to the office, I'll make us some coffee."

As they walked toward the back of the store, Colette was aware of his gaze darting here and there, taking in the displays, the furniture and various items they passed.

Colette was proud of the layout of the store. She'd spent long hours and utilized all her marketing training in order to create a store that would be comfortable to shop in and displays that would encourage spending.

"What's all this?" he asked as they passed a large area at the back of the store that was empty except for several sawhorses and some tools.

"I'm having a little kiddy area built back here. It's going to have little benches and tables with books and puzzles. Lots of my customers come in with children, and I thought it would be great to have a place for those children to play while their parents shopped.''

''Very thoughtful,'' he said.

She grinned. ''Business thoughtful. Parents tend to spend more time shopping if they don't have children whining or hanging on them. And the more time people spend shopping, the more they are apt to spend.''

She gestured him into the business office. She'd always believed the office at the back of the store was large, but the moment Tanner followed her in, she felt as if the interior had significantly shrunk.

''Please, have a seat.'' She motioned him to the chair in front of her desk, then went to the corner where there was a sink and a counter with the coffeepot on top.

It took her only moments to prepare the coffeepot and turn it on. She sat down at her desk, fighting a sudden, irrational nervousness as the scent of the fresh brew filled the air.

It had been easy to spend time with Tanner the night before with Gina there. But at the moment she felt ill at ease, and was far too aware of him not as Gina's brother, but as a very sexy, single man. A man who, according to Gina, didn't have a girlfriend because he was so stubborn.

He didn't speak until they each had a cup of coffee before them and she had opened the bag and offered him a bagel. "I assume from your store that you like babies," he said.

"I love babies," she replied easily. "But that's not why I decided to sell baby items." He crooked a dark eyebrow in obvious interest, and she continued. "I knew I wanted to open my own retail business and it took me several months to finally decide on the baby business."

"So why babies?"

"I studied the markets, did exhaustive research and realized we are on the verge of another baby boom. That, coupled with the fact that no matter what the economy is like, people are always going to have babies."

"That's very interesting," he said. "So, your decision was based on intellect rather than emotion."

Something in his tone hinted of disapproval and Colette raised her chin defensively. "It's been my experience that the best decisions you can make are ones made with your mind, not with your heart. But surely you know that. When you chose what kind of cows to raise, I'm sure you made that decision with your head, not your heart."

He grinned, that lazy, sexy grin that instantly put her on edge. "It's difficult to get too emotional over a cow."

Colette tore off a piece of bagel and ate it, then took a sip of her coffee, desperately trying to think of something to talk about. She certainly didn't want to discuss the situation with Gina with him. She didn't want to get involved in a tug-of-war between a brother and sister.

"Gina tells me you are from a very small town in Kansas," she finally said.

He nodded. "Foxrun, Kansas. It's more like a little neighborhood than a town. Everyone knows everyone else, and most of the time everyone knows everyone else's business."

She smiled. "Sounds like fun."

"I can't imagine living anywhere else."

"Do your parents live there, as well?"

His blue eyes grew deeper in color and Colette thought she saw a whisper of pain in their depths. He looked down at the coffee mug in his hands. "My parents have been gone for a long time. They died in a car accident when I was twenty-one years old and Gina was ten. I was left with a ranch on the verge of financial ruin and a ten-year-old grief-stricken child."

Suddenly Colette understood his overprotectiveness where Gina was concerned. He'd not only been big brother to her, he'd also been mother and father. Admiration for him filled her.

No wonder he was having problems letting go of her. Colette knew there were parents who had trouble letting go of their children, although her mother certainly had not been that kind of parent.

"It must have been very difficult for you," she said

softly. "Twenty-one is terribly young to take on so much responsibility and work."

"In the case of both the ranch and Gina, it was definitely a labor of love."

The warmth in his eyes and the soft expression on his face stirred a strange longing in Colette. Confused by the odd emotion, she stood and walked over to the coffeemaker to refill her cup.

When she turned back around she caught his gaze sweeping over her, taking in the sum total of her from head to toe. She suddenly wondered if her skirt was too short or too tight. She fought against the blush that tried to take possession of her cheeks and returned to her seat behind the desk.

"So, tell me about Colette Carson," he said, then took another sip of his coffee.

She shrugged. "There really isn't much to tell. I was born and raised right here in Kansas City and have been here all my life."

"Is there a boyfriend in the picture? An attractive woman like you probably dates every night." His eyes flashed with what she thought might be a flirtatious light.

She laughed, oddly pleased that he thought she was attractive. "I can't remember the last date I had." He was probably wondering how many nights a week his sister spent alone in the apartment. "Most evenings I'm either looking at catalogs, trying to figure out what might be the next hot item, or going over the books to see exactly how the shop is doing. Gina tells me you don't do much dating, either.''

"Like you, it's difficult to find the time.''

Colette grinned teasingly. "That's not what Gina says. She said you don't have a girlfriend because you're too mean and stubborn. I believe her exact term was 'cursedly stubborn.'''

He laughed, a deep rumbling sound that was pleasant. "She's probably right. I've been known to be pretty bullheaded. Still, it seems a shame that a pretty girl like you spends all her time on business. How are you going to find Mr. Right if you don't date?'' Again his eyes were filled with a light that unsettled her yet shot a streak of heat through her.

"Finding Mr. Right has never been a priority of mine,'' she replied.

With his million-dollar smile warming her, and his overwhelmingly masculine presence filling the office, Colette felt a sudden need to escape.

She looked at her watch and stood. "It's time for me to open up the shop,'' she said, although it was still earlier than her usual opening time. "You're welcome to stay here and finish your bagel and coffee or whatever. As I told you earlier, Gina doesn't come in until noon.''

She was aware of his gaze sweeping the length of her as she headed for the door that led out into the shop. "If you don't mind, I'll just finish up my coffee back here,'' he said.

Nodding, she fled the office, grateful to get some distance from him. Although she had certainly admired his attractiveness and charm the night before, she hadn't felt the utter magnitude of his sexual appeal the way she had this morning.

She unlocked the front door and flipped the Closed sign to Open, then walked over to the chair behind the small counter that held the cash register.

She had the distinct impression that he'd been subtly flirting with her when he'd spoken about her dating habits, and her pulse had accelerated to an uncomfortable pace.

As she greeted her first customer of the day, she remembered Gina's words of warning about Tanner. She'd warned Colette not to be fooled by his charm, and Colette realized she would do well to take heed.

She did find Tanner charming, and although she had never felt herself particularly susceptible to any man's charm, she had a feeling if she allowed it, Tanner Rothman could definitely be a threat to the carefully controlled, safe life she'd built for herself.

Tanner knew she'd expected him to leave after he finished his coffee and to return later when Gina arrived for work, but instead he rinsed out the cup, then joined her at the counter out front.

He leaned against a back wall, watching as she took care of a pregnant woman who looked about ready to burst open like a ripe watermelon.

Tanner had never thought much about having children of his own. At the time when most men began thinking of having families, he'd been busy raising Gina. Now, at thirty-two years old, he almost felt as if it were too late to think about babies of his own.

He redirected his gaze to Colette. Again this morning she was dressed in a three-piece suit. The deep gray jacket was short and fitted over a crisp white blouse, and the skirt was pencil thin and short enough to display her long, slender but shapely legs.

It hadn't taken long into their conversation for his suspicions about Colette Carson to be confirmed. She was certainly not the kind of woman he wanted as a role model for his impressionable sister.

Despite the fact she had dynamite legs and the longest, darkest eyelashes he'd ever seen. In spite of the fact that she had the sweet features of an angel and a body that would make most red-blooded men think of sin, he had the feeling she was a cold, heartless woman driven by ambition.

He'd been vaguely disappointed when she'd told him why she'd decided to open a shop selling baby items. Although it appeared to have been a smart decision, he was disappointed that the decision was made strictly from a business perspective.

Gina had lacked a female role model in her life. There had been no aunts, no godmother, nobody to step into the void the loss of their mother had created in Gina's life.

Colette was a distinctive threat to all that he wanted for Gina's future. He certainly didn't want Gina to emulate a hard-driven ambitious woman who, he suspected, didn't have much of a heart.

Still, he couldn't help but feel a grudging admiration for Colette as he watched her working with the customers who came in...and there was a steady stream of customers.

She was courteous, respectful and infinitely patient with every shopper. He also couldn't help but admire the natural grace with which she moved as she guided customers from display to display.

He could tell she was surprised that he was hanging around. As she attended to her customers, her gaze continually sought him.

Maybe by hanging around long enough he'd irritate her and she would decide that Gina was more trouble than she was worth. Then she'd join him in the war to get Gina to return home.

"I never knew there could be so many expectant parents in one city," he said when there was a lull in the customers.

She smiled and straightened the blankets in one of the cribs on display. "Not everyone who comes in is expecting a baby. Friends and relatives of expectant or new parents come in to find a gift for the birth or for a shower."

She gave the blanket a final pat, then straightened. "But this has all got to be terribly boring for you."

"Not at all. Is Gina as good a salesman as you are?"

Colette smiled and Tanner felt a renewed tug of attraction. "She's a great salesclerk."

"Is Gina your only employee?" It would require ridiculously long hours for only two people to run the store.

"I have two other women who work for me on a part-time basis," she replied. "But Gina is my only full-time worker." She smiled and excused herself as another customer came through the door.

Tanner resumed his position against the back wall, surprised when a few minutes later Gina came through the shop door. He was shocked to realize he'd been standing around and watching Colette work for the past several hours.

"How long have you been here?" Gina asked suspiciously.

"Why?" he countered.

She set her purse behind the counter and looked over to where Colette was showing a couple of expectant parents the variety of cribs she carried.

"I was wondering how long you've had to try to get Colette on your side."

He grinned. "I got here before she opened the store and we shared bagels and coffee. And I'll have you know we didn't even discuss you."

Gina looked surprised. "Then what did you talk about?"

"This and that," he replied.

Gina's eyes narrowed. "I know you, Tanner Rothman. You never do anything without a reason. Colette is my friend and my roommate, and you just leave her out of this."

"Gina." Tanner took one of his sister's hands in his. "Come home. You were less than a year away from your teaching degree. Come home and finish up college, stay at the ranch until you get married and have a family of your own. You don't want to be a store clerk for the rest of your life."

"I don't want to go back to Foxrun. I like it here," she protested. "And I'm not going to be a store clerk for the rest of my life. Colette is starting to train me as a manager and a buyer." She pulled her hand out of his and went to greet a customer who had just come through the front door.

Tanner sighed in frustration and looked back over to Colette. As he gazed at her, Gina's words replayed in his mind. "She's my friend and my roommate, and you just leave her out of this."

He couldn't very well leave Colette out of it. She was smack-dab in the middle, making promises to Gina that undermined what Tanner wanted.

As lovely as she was, as desirable as he found her, he couldn't forget that she was the enemy. And what he intended to do was seduce the enemy and bring her to his side of the war.

Chapter Three

To say that Tanner Rothman was a distraction was a vast understatement. His overwhelming presence filled the store, and no matter where she stood, she thought she could smell his evocative scent.

He was too tall, his shoulders far too broad, and his utter masculinity and sexiness made it difficult for Colette to focus on work.

Between customers he visited with both Gina and her, charming Colette with his funny stories of ranch life and tidbits from Gina's childhood.

Even Gina seemed to loosen up as her brother regaled them with charming stories of small-town life. The love between brother and sister was palpable in the air, and Colette found herself wishing she'd had somebody like Tanner Rothman in her life. And the more appealing she found Tanner Rothman, the more uncomfortable she felt.

By the time six o'clock came and Linda Craig, one of the part-time workers, came to relieve Colette, she was more than ready to get away from Tanner.

She wasn't sure why he affected her on such a physical level. She didn't understand why his nearness made her breath catch in her chest and turned her palms slightly sweaty.

She'd been intensely aware of his midnight-blue gaze lingering on her often throughout the day. Each time she'd been aware of his gaze, her insides had quivered.

She'd been intimate with one man in her life. She'd dated Mike Covington for three months before she'd finally slept with him. The experience hadn't been particularly overwhelming, and that's why she didn't understand her almost primal response to Tanner.

Sex had never been important to her, but Tanner made her think of sex...of tangled sheets and hot slick bodies, and of slightly callused hands running down the length of her body. He made her think thoughts she rarely entertained.

Stepping out of the store, she drew a deep breath. It had been a good sales day, and she had evening plans of sitting down with a catalog and picking out the baby items she wanted for the baby she might be carrying at this very moment.

She figured Gina would only be with her for a couple of months and would then find her own place, leaving Gina's bedroom as a nursery. Colette intended to make it a showcase of a room, a place where dreams could be nurtured.

She'd only taken two or three steps away from the shop when the door flew open and Tanner joined her on the sidewalk. "Thought I'd walk you home," he said as he fell into step at her side. "It doesn't seem right to let a pretty lady walk home on the mean streets of the city all alone." He gestured toward the stack of catalogs in her arms. "What me to carry your books home from school?"

She laughed, her pulse quickening. "No, but thanks anyway. And I've been walking the mean city streets alone for the past ten years, ever since I was eighteen years old."

"Well, while I'm in town, you aren't going to be doing it anymore," he replied.

"Aren't you the gallant one," she said teasingly.

"Gina would call it overly protective," he said with a half scowl.

Colette laughed, surprised to discover she was glad he'd decided to walk her home. "Gina is young. All she believes is that you're here to rain on her parade."

"But I'm not," he replied, his blue eyes sparkling earnestly. "Three weeks ago Gina and I had a fight. It was a silly argument and I didn't think too much about it at the time. She packed a bag, told me she was leaving Foxrun and drove off. I figured she'd be home by nightfall.''

"But she wasn't," Colette said. She tried not to notice how the bright sunshine made his dark hair gleam with richness.

"No, she wasn't. I waited until the next afternoon, then began to ask questions of friends and neighbors. That's when I discovered Margaret Jamison had a friend in Kansas City and had encouraged Gina to come here." The muscle in his jaw tightened in obvious irritation.

"I gather Margaret Jamison isn't one of your favorite people right now."

The muscle ticked again. "I think she's a busybody who should keep her nose to her own business." A slight flush swept up his neck. "Sorry, I shouldn't have said that. I know she's your friend."

"She's also a busybody," Colette agreed with a small laugh. "But she means well. She worked for me in the shop for about six months before her husband bought the farm out west." They stopped in front of her apartment building.

"They bought the place right next door to mine," Tanner replied. He swept a hand through his rich dark hair and frowned thoughtfully. "Anyway, it was Margaret who told me about you, said she'd talked to you about you hiring Gina and giving her a place to stay for a while."

Colette nodded. "Margaret called me and told me

that Gina was a sweet, bright young woman ready to strike out on her own.''

"She is sweet and she is bright, but she is also incredibly naive and innocent and not prepared for life on her own. She's never even had a real job before.''

"But she told me she did volunteer work at an animal shelter and at the local hospital.'' Colette juggled the catalogs into one of her arms and with the other hand retrieved her keys. "Tanner, I really don't want to get in the middle of this fight between you and Gina. This should be a decision the two of you make.''

"You're right,'' he said instantly. "I'm sorry, I shouldn't have brought it up.''

Colette hesitated, knowing she shouldn't say any more but unable to help herself. "All I know for sure is that in the three weeks Gina has been working for me, she's proven herself to be very conscientious and responsible. Maybe it's possible you're seeing her as the little girl she was instead of the young woman she's become.''

His eyes grew stormy and the tic once again pounded in his jawline. "I know what's best for her. And it's best she come back to Foxrun with me.'' His voice rang with an authority she hadn't heard before.

"Then I guess all you have to do is convince her of that,'' Colette replied. "And now, if you'll excuse me, I'm going to get settled in for the night.''

"Yes, of course." He smiled, but she could tell the pleasant gesture was forced. "I'll see you tomorrow."

Colette watched him as he turned and walked away. He walked with a loose-hipped gait that held a touch of arrogance.

She turned and went into her building. As she rode the elevator up to the eighth floor, she thought of the conversation they'd just had.

In the last moments of that conversation she'd seen a flash of the man Gina had described to her—a man determined to have his own way. She had a feeling that beneath his obvious charm was a man who could truly be "cursedly stubborn."

Entering her apartment, she immediately kicked off her shoes, dropped the catalogs on the coffee table and then went into the bedroom to change her clothes.

On the one hand she was taken with the obvious love Tanner felt for his sister, the worry and concern she knew had driven him to the city in pursuit of her. On the other hand she had a feeling he was vastly underestimating Gina's strength and resolve.

She had just finished changing her clothes when the phone rang. Flopping on the bed, she picked up the phone on the nightstand.

"Colette, I'm glad I caught you in."

"Hello, Lillian," Colette said to her mother.

"I got the message that you called last week and thought I would return your call."

Colette wanted to say that it was a good thing she

hadn't called with an emergency, but she'd long ago realized her mother was incapable of giving the emotions and love Colette had once hungered for.

"Mother's Day is next Sunday. I was wondering if you'd like to go to lunch with me?" Colette twisted the phone cord around her finger as she realized how much she would love it if her mother said yes.

"I'm afraid I can't," Lillian replied, no regret in her voice at all. "Joe and I have planned a little mini-trip for the weekend. You know how he loves to fish."

No, Colette didn't know. She knew very little about Joe Kinsell, her mother's latest boy-toy. She'd only met him once.

"Well, that's nice. I hope the two of you have a wonderful time," she said, unwrapping the cord from her hand.

"Oh, I'm sure we will. We always have a wonderful time together. We need you to come over here and feed and take care of Cuddles." Cuddles was her mother's poodle.

Colette wondered if her mother hadn't needed to talk to her about caring for Cuddles, if she would have called at all.

"Of course. I'll be glad to."

"Good. We'll be back late Sunday night and I'll call you sometime next week when things quiet down again." With these words, Lillian disconnected.

As Colette hung up the phone, a painful emptiness

resounded in her heart. She should be used to the fact that she wasn't on her mother's list of priorities. She never had been. She'd learned very early not to need anyone, not to depend on anyone other than herself.

She rolled over on her back and placed a hand on her tummy. She'd never wanted anything as much as she wanted a baby. And the thought that at this very moment she might be pregnant filled her with a sweet warmth that banished the emptiness of moments before.

Although she'd been told that it might take several attempts for the artificial insemination to succeed, she was hoping she'd be one of the lucky ones and the first attempt had been successful.

Thoughts of Tanner and Gina once again filled her head. They were so lucky to have each other. But she had a feeling it wouldn't be long before she felt as if she was in the middle of a war zone. She wondered how long she could remain neutral, and if eventually she had to choose a side, which side would she choose?

As Tanner walked back to the store, he couldn't remember a time when he'd felt so energized, and he knew what the feeling was—sexual tension.

He wasn't even sure if he liked Colette Carson, but he knew damn straight he wanted her. It was crazy, it was utterly irrational, but it was there…thrumming through his veins, reminding him of just how long it had been since he'd been intimate with a woman.

Too long. When Gina had been younger, Tanner had wanted to set a good example for her and had never had a woman to the ranch. He hadn't started dating until recently, but had found no woman he particularly wanted to be intimate with.

Again and again throughout the course of the day he'd found his gaze drawn to Colette. He'd found himself wondering what her lips would taste like? If her skin was really as silky to the touch as it looked as if it would be?

His desire for her had nothing to do with his desire to make her see his side of the issue with Gina. They were two very separate issues—one using his head, and the other utilizing a visceral part of him that had little to do with his mind.

As he walked through the shop door, all thoughts of Colette blew out of his mind as he saw his sister leaning over the counter obviously flirting with a young man wearing a delivery uniform.

She straightened as she saw Tanner. "Tanner, I'd like you to meet Danny Burlington. Danny, this is my brother, Tanner Rothman."

The young man held a hand out to Tanner. Tanner grasped it and gave it a shake. "You here making a delivery or trying to pick something up?"

"Tanner!" Gina exclaimed angrily.

Danny released Tanner's hand, but held his gaze.

"I'm here to visit with Gina, sir. In fact, I've asked her to go to a late dinner with me this evening and perhaps see a movie."

"And I've told him I'd be delighted to go with him," Gina exclaimed. Her expression warned Tanner, and he suddenly realized that if he handled this situation the way he wanted to, he'd risk losing Gina forever.

He placed an arm around Gina and forced a smile to his lips as he looked at Danny. "I trust you'll make it a relatively early night since Gina is a working woman."

Danny visibly relaxed. "Yes, sir. I start my job early in the mornings, too. We won't make it a late night."

Tanner decided it would be better if he didn't ask for a copy of Danny's driver's license or get fingerprints from the young man, although that's exactly what he wanted to do.

"Come on, Danny. I'll walk you out," Gina said. She slithered out from beneath Tanner's arm and walked with Danny to the door.

Tanner watched his sister as she smiled up at the handsome delivery boy. This was just what he'd feared...that she'd be swept off her feet by a sweet-talking city slicker.

At worst, he'd leave her pregnant and alone. At best, she'd fancy herself in love with him and never agree to return to the ranch with Tanner.

Still, as much as he wanted to rant and rave and call off her date, he couldn't. He knew that the way he handled this latest crisis would either lead to his ultimate success in gaining what he wanted or doom him to failure.

He forced a smile at Linda, the part-time worker who had come in just before he'd walked Colette home. She glared at him, then returned to folding baby blankets. He wondered what his baby sister had told her about him? Somehow he knew by her glare that whatever Gina had said had not been too favorable.

Gina smiled, her eyes sparkling as she came back into the shop. "Thank you," she said as she got to where Tanner stood.

"For what?"

"For not being mean and hateful to Danny." She leaned her elbows on the counter, her features retaining her smile. "He's been really nice to me since I came to Kansas City. Most evenings he comes here to walk me home after I close up the store. I told him he didn't have to tonight because you're here."

Tanner shoved his hands in his jeans, fighting the impulse to reach out and grab her to his chest, hold her tight and keep her safe from life. "So what do you know about him?" he asked, trying to keep his tone light.

She shrugged and walked over to a nearby display of baby shoes. "I know he's twenty-five years old and has been working for the delivery company for four years,'' she said as she straightened the boxes of shoes. "He lives with his family not far from here and has two younger sisters and a little brother.''

Tanner felt somewhat better knowing Danny didn't have a place of his own. If he took her back to his house, with three siblings and parents, it would probably be difficult to sneak in anything more than a kiss or two.

"Now, tell me, big brother, what do you think about my roommate. She's nice, isn't she?''

"She's all right,'' Tanner replied.

Gina gave him a sly smile. "I saw the way you looked at her all day. I'd say you thought she was better than all right.''

Tanner was shocked to feel a slight flush of heat rising up his neck. "I don't know what you're talking about,'' he muttered.

"Oh, Tanner.'' She danced back over to him and put her slender arms around his neck. "Don't you realize that my independence is also yours? You've given the best years of your life to raising me. Now it's time to get on with your own life.''

Tanner gave her a hug but didn't mention the fact that it wasn't time for her independence yet. She was a baby bird not yet ready to fly from the nest, and he was determined to catch her before she fell.

Two hours later he walked Gina home through the

deepening shadows of twilight. "I hate the idea of you walking home alone in the evenings," he said.

"I told you, most nights Danny walks me home."

"But what about the nights that he doesn't?"

She sighed with a touch of impatience. "Then I walk home quickly with my head held high. Colette says if you don't look like a victim, then the odds are good you won't become one. And just to be on the safe side, I carry pepper spray in my purse."

"Nobody ever has to carry pepper spray in Foxrun," he observed.

"That's because nothing ever happens in Foxrun," she replied, as if it were a bad thing. "It's a nice little town filled with nice people, but I want more than Foxrun can give me."

They stopped in front of the apartment building. She gazed up at him thoughtfully. "Since I'm having dinner with Danny, why don't you invite Colette out for some dinner?"

He raised an eyebrow in surprise. "I thought you didn't want me consorting with your roommate and boss." He smiled teasingly. "I thought you had some sort of a conspiracy theory going...you know, you believe I'm trying to sway her to my side of the argument."

"I was worried about that," she replied. "But after giving it some thought, I've decided you and Colette hanging out together isn't a threat to me."

"And why is that?" he asked indulgently.

"Colette is the strongest most independent woman I know. From what I know about her, she's never depended on anyone and has already accomplished so much all on her own. I think she knows my dreams are a lot like hers and she's going to support me in what I want to do." She grinned at him impishly. "And I don't think even the famous Tanner charm can make her work against me."

He returned her grin. "Perhaps you're underestimating the power of the famous Tanner charm."

"Maybe I am," she agreed soberly. "In any case, I'm having dinner with Danny and I just thought you'd rather eat with Colette than eat alone."

Tanner eyed his sister suspiciously. He didn't trust this sudden change of heart of hers. Earlier in the day she'd been rabid about telling him to stay away from Colette. Now she seemed to be giving him an open invitation to pursue his plot to get Colette on his side and manipulate Gina into coming back home.

"Maybe I *will* see if Colette wants to get a bite to eat with me," he said.

Together he and Gina got into the elevator that carried them to the eighth-floor apartment. It intrigued Tanner, how the thought of having dinner with Colette filled him with a strange sense of anticipation.

He followed Gina through the front door and instantly saw Colette. Clad in what was obviously a short, cotton nightshirt, she was curled up on the sofa with a stack of catalogs on the coffee table in front of her.

It was obvious she had recently showered. Her hair was in damp curls, and her face had a fresh-scrubbed glow that made Tanner's fingers itch to stroke her creamy-looking cheeks.

It was also obvious she hadn't expected him to come in with Gina. The nightshirt, although loose fitting, was thin, and he could see the thrust of her breasts against the pink material. A wave of desire swept through him, bringing with it a sweet flood of heat that suffused his entire body.

"Tanner," she exclaimed and half rose from the sofa, at the same time tugging self-consciously at the bottom of the nightshirt. "I wasn't expecting—" She finally sat and put her feet demurely together on the floor.

"Please, don't get up," he said. "I'm not staying. I just walked Gina home." He remained standing by the front door.

"I've got a date and Tanner was going to invite you to eat dinner with him, but it looks like you've already eaten." Gina gestured to the remains of a microwave dinner that sat next to a stack of catalogs.

"Yes...I already ate."

Tanner thought he heard a touch of disappointment in her voice and was surprised to find that he was disappointed, too.

He told himself it was because he'd wanted an opportunity to sway Colette to his way of thinking, that if he could get her on his side, perhaps he could talk her into firing Gina and making her move out of the apartment. Then Gina would have no other choice than to return home.

Colette looked at Gina once again. "You have a date?"

Gina grinned, her eyes sparkling once again. "With Danny."

"Oh, Gina. That's wonderful! I know how much you've been hoping he'd ask you out!"

Colette jumped up off the sofa and hugged Gina, the motion giving Tanner a tantalizing view of creamy thighs. He shifted from foot to foot and looked away, fighting a renewed burst of heat that stole through his body.

"Well, then, I'll just get out of here," he said, his voice breaking the two women apart. Once again Colette sat down, her cheeks slightly pink as if she was aware that she was inappropriately dressed for company.

"Good night, Tanner. Sorry about dinner," she replied.

He nodded, then looked at his sister. "Please, call my hotel room when you get home tonight so I'll know you got back safely."

"Oh, Tanner...honestly." Gina rolled her eyes.

"It sounds like a simple enough request," Colette said, and Tanner sent her a smile of gratitude.

"All right, all right. I'll call you when I get in,"
Gina agreed with a sigh of exasperation.

"Thank you," Tanner replied, and kissed her on
her forehead. He cast one final look at Colette, wondering how he was going to spend the hours of Gina's
date and why he wished he could spend them on the
sofa with her roommate.

Chapter Four

It was after eleven when Colette got out of bed for a drink of water and thought she heard something, or someone, just outside her apartment door.

At first she thought it might be Danny and Gina arriving home from their date. She looked out the peephole and spied a very tiny Tanner leaning against the wall opposite her apartment door.

What on earth was he doing out there? In an instant the answer sprang to her mind. Dear God, the man was waiting for Gina to get home from her date.

Gina would be positively horrified when she arrived back at the apartment with Danny and discovered big brother lurking in the hallway.

She went back into her bedroom and pulled on a floor-length cotton robe, then went back to the front door and opened it.

"Tanner? Please don't tell me you're here for the reason I think you're here."

"Okay. Why do you think I'm here?"

"I think you're here to spy on your sister."

He grinned, obviously undaunted by her accusation. "Not spy," he protested. "I just figured I'd see for myself that she got home safe and sound."

Colette shook her head with a rueful smile. "I can't believe you. At least come inside and wait for her. She'll never forgive you if she comes home and finds you lurking in the hallway."

He hesitated. "Are you sure? I mean, it is rather late and I don't want to bother you."

"I'm already bothered with a case of insomnia. Come on in and I'll fix us some coffee." As usual, she was intensely aware of him as he followed her through the living room and into the kitchen.

She motioned him to the kitchen table, unable to help but notice that his big, bold presence seemed to overwhelm the glass-and-brass dinette set.

"Excuse me if it's none of my business," she began as she quickly got the coffeemaker prepared. "But hasn't Gina gone on dates before tonight?"

"Of course," he exclaimed. "She started dating when she was about seventeen."

"Then what are you so nervous about?"

As the coffee began to gurgle into the glass container, she turned back to face him, although she didn't move to join him at the table.

"The guys Gina was dating back home I knew. I'd watched them grow up, I knew their families," he explained. "And they knew me and knew that if they stepped out of line with her, they'd have to answer to me."

"And that was a daunting prospect?" she asked teasingly.

He grinned, that sexy slow curve of his lips that sent a starburst of heat exploding in the pit of her stomach. "That's what I've been told."

She turned toward the cabinets and took down two mugs, grateful for the physical activity to take her mind off that smile of his. "Cream or sugar?" she asked.

"Just black is fine."

She poured them each a cup of the fresh brew, then turned back to face him. The thought of sitting next to him at the table suddenly seemed overwhelming. The table was too small. Heck, the entire kitchen was too small. "Why don't we take this back into the living room?" she suggested.

"Okay." He stood and walked over to her. He stood so close to her she could feel his body heat, smell the scent of him that caused a crazy tickling in her tummy. "Why don't you let me carry those?" He gestured to the mugs in her hands.

"No, that's fine. I've got them." She stepped away and headed into the living room, intensely aware of him just behind her. She set one of the mugs on the coffee table, then carried the other one to the chair and sat.

Tanner eased down onto the sofa and wrapped his big hands around the mug. "So what do you think about this Danny that Gina is out with?"

Colette smiled. "I really don't think you have anything to be worried about. He seems to be a very nice kid. He and Gina started making eyes at each other the first day she started work for me and he made a delivery. Then, about a week and a half ago he started showing up to walk her home from work. It's been rather sweet to watch a bit of romance blooming between them."

He frowned and took a sip of his coffee. "Gina is too young to get involved with any man."

Colette hesitated a moment, then nodded. "I agree that I'd hate to see her get real serious about somebody at this age. I think it's important that women establish themselves and their independence before deciding to get into a serious relationship with a man."

One of his dark eyebrows lifted. "Is that what you're doing? Waiting until you have firmly established your independence before getting into a relationship with a man?"

"I've been independent for a very long time," she replied. "And I really have no desire, no need, for a man in my life. I like depending only on myself."

"That can get pretty lonely," he observed.

She thought of the baby she might be carrying. She wouldn't be lonely ever again if she had a child. "I don't have time to get lonely."

"Back home in Foxrun, you'd be considered real unnatural."

Colette eyed him in surprise. "Unnatural? My goodness, why?"

He grinned. "Most of the single women in Foxrun want only one thing—to find a good man. They don't care about independence. They want to be half of a couple."

She laughed. "Then as far as I'm concerned, they are misguided souls."

"You mentioned before that you'd been on your own since you were eighteen. That's pretty young." He took another sip of his coffee.

She smiled. "If Lillian had had her way, I'd have been out on my own when I was six."

"Lillian?"

"My mother," she explained.

He leaned back against the cushions, the beige sofa a perfect foil for his dark handsomeness. "You call your mother by her first name?"

She nodded. "When I was ten my mother insisted I stop calling her 'mother' and start calling her Lillian. She didn't want people to know that she was old enough to have a daughter my age."

"So, basically you lost your mother when you were ten years old, just like Gina did."

She looked at him in surprise. "I never really thought about it like that before."

"What about your father? Has he passed on?"

"Who knows. I never knew him. He and my mother were never married, and he left her when I was about six months old. I was raised with a succession of 'uncles.' My mother is one of those women who can't seem to be alone."

Tanner finished his coffee, then looked at his watch and frowned. "It's after midnight. What could they be doing?" He stood and walked over to the window and stared out.

"Tanner, Danny didn't pick her up until almost nine. By the time they get something to eat and see a movie it will probably be close to one before they get back here."

He turned from the window and raked a hand through his hair. "Did you know Gina only had one more year of college left, then she would have her teaching degree?"

"No, I didn't know that. I always wished I'd had a chance to go to college and get a degree." She frowned thoughtfully, again wondering if Gina really knew what she was turning her back on in her bid to gain some freedom. She stood and gestured to his coffee cup. "Would you like some more?"

"No, thanks." He picked up his cup and followed her into the kitchen. He leaned against the counter as she turned off the coffeepot and placed their mugs into the dishwasher.

When she turned back to face him, there was a glow in his eyes that set her on edge, a sexy look that made her heart step up its rhythm.

"You're staring at me," she said with a breathless, embarrassed laugh.

"Sorry." He took a step closer to her. "I was just thinking about why I was so worried about Gina being out on a date."

"And why is that?" She wanted him to step back. She wanted him to step closer. There was an energy in the air between them, an energy that sparkled and snapped with electric currents.

"Because I know what goes through guys' minds when they are with a pretty woman. Because those kinds of things are going through my mind right now."

Colette's heart thrummed frantically as he reached up and touched the side of her face with his index finger. "And what kinds of things are those?" she asked, her voice even more breathless than before.

His finger moved from her cheek and skimmed across her lower lip. Colette felt as if her knees might buckle at any moment. "What's going through my mind right now is that I'm wondering if the area just behind your ear is sensitive."

His breath was a warm caress on her face as he took a step closer to her. "I'm wondering if your skin is soft to the touch and if your lips will taste as sweet as they look.''

''I guess there's only one way to find out,'' she said, surprising herself with her own boldness.

His eyes glowed more brightly as he recognized her words as an invitation. He wasted no time but dipped his head to claim her lips with his own.

Instantly Colette realized not only was this man devastatingly handsome and sexy, but he was a master at kissing, as well. His mouth was soft, gentle at first. Then his arms wrapped around her and he pulled her against him, deepening the kiss by touching his tongue to hers.

The sensations that coursed through her were breath stealing. His mouth was a volcano of heat, his chest a solid wall of rock-hard muscle against the press of her breasts.

She lost all sense of herself as his mouth continued to ply hers with heat and their tongues swirled erotically against one another.

His arms wrapped her tight, and for a brief, crazy moment she felt more safe than she ever had in her life. His mouth left her lips and sought the sensitive skin just behind her ear. A shiver of delight raced through her at the erotic touch of his tongue and his warm breath in her ear.

''Colette?'' Gina's voice rang out from the living room. Tanner and Colette flew apart just as she walked into the kitchen.

"Tanner...what are you doing here?" She looked from Tanner to Colette, then back again at her brother.

"Tanner came by to see if you were home yet, and we just had a cup of coffee and chatted a bit. There's some coffee left if you'd like a cup. I only shut it off a minute ago. It should still be warm." Colette knew she was rambling, and she hoped her lips didn't look as swollen as they felt, hoped that Gina had no clue that what they'd been doing was indulging in a mind-blowing kiss that had swept all sense from Colette's head.

"No, no coffee for me," Gina said, and stifled a yawn with the back of her hand. "You see, I'm home safe and sound, so you can go back to your hotel now," Gina said to Tanner. "I'm going to bed. I'll talk to you both in the morning." She left them standing in the kitchen.

"I told you she'd be fine," Colette said as she belted her robe more tightly around her waist. "And now I need to get some sleep, as well." She needed him to leave, needed to get away from him.

Her mouth still tingled with the imprint of his, and there was nothing she wanted to do more than repeat their kiss. And that frightened her.

"Then I guess I'll see you tomorrow," he said as they walked from the kitchen to the front door.

"I guess so," she agreed, slightly embarrassed now that the mood of moments before had passed.

He hesitated at the door and she could tell by his expression that he wanted to say something more. "Good night, Tanner," she said to preempt anything he might want to say. She opened the door, her gaze not meeting his.

"Good night, Colette." He looked at her another long moment, then turned and left.

She closed the door after him, then locked it and leaned against it. She had to stay away from Tanner Rothman. He was a definite threat to all that she had worked so hard to achieve, all the personal strength she had gained as an adult.

For just a moment, as he'd held her in his arms and kissed her so sweetly, so deeply, she'd felt weak and incredibly needy. For that reason alone he was to be avoided at all costs.

Tanner stepped out into the late-night air and drew a deep breath. Colette. Her scent clung to his skin, and the taste of her mouth still filled his.

Kissing her had been a big mistake, for in doing so he'd awakened hormones that had lain dormant for a long time. It had also confirmed his suspicions— her lips were just as soft and sweet as he'd suspected.

What he hadn't expected was the all-consuming heat that had filled him as he'd held her in his arms, as he'd kissed her lips.

He frowned thoughtfully as he walked back to his

hotel. Colette Carson stood for everything he didn't want in a woman.

She was obviously intensely independent, didn't have a clue what it was like to be part of a real family and was subtly encouraging his sister to be just like her.

Yet even recognizing all that, he wanted to hold her again. He wanted to kiss her again.

He was still feeling the same conflicting emotions the next afternoon when he arrived at the Little Bit Baby Boutique. He'd specifically waited until after noon to arrive, knowing that by then Gina would be there.

After all, his reason for being in Kansas City had nothing to do with the lovely Colette Carson and everything to do with his sister. He needed to focus his energies on getting Gina back to the ranch, not on figuring out how soon he could kiss Colette again.

Almost the minute he walked into the shop, Colette excused herself and headed out to lunch. He fought the impulse to invite himself along, realizing the time alone with Gina would be a perfect opportunity to step up his campaign to get her home.

"I didn't get a chance to ask you last night. How was your big date?" he asked when Colette was gone and it was just he and Gina in the store. They were seated side by side on chairs just behind the cash register counter.

"Oh, it was wonderful," Gina exclaimed. "We

went and saw the new Jackie Chan movie, and it was so funny we laughed until we were in tears. That man is so talented and he has a face that just makes you smile when you look at him.''

"I'm less interested in how you feel about Jackie Chan than in how you feel about Danny," Tanner said dryly.

Gina smiled. "Danny is sweet and fun and I like him a lot," she replied.

"I hope you don't like him too much," Tanner replied, an edge of worry rising up inside him. Eventually he wanted to see Gina happily married and with a family of her own. But he didn't want her to hurry things. "Gina...we never really talked about men and women and stuff." He struggled to find the right words to tell her what he felt needed to be said.

"Oh, Tanner...please. Don't tell me you're going to try to have *that* talk with me now."

"*That* talk?"

"You know...the birds and the bees talk." A slight stain of color reddened Gina's cheeks.

Embarrassment stole through Tanner, as well. "I probably should have had that talk with you a while ago," he began.

"Yeah, like in seventh grade. It's a little late now, Tanner. I learned everything I needed to know from Maggie Christian's mom."

"You did?"

Although her cheeks remained pink, Gina smiled

at her brother. "Tanner, I know all about sexually transmitted diseases. I know what makes babies and how to prevent both diseases and pregnancy."

"That's not all I worry about," Tanner replied. "I mean, I'd hate for you to get too serious too fast," he added.

She looked at him in surprise. "Is that what you're worried about? That I'll fall in love with Danny and get married right away?" She laughed and shook her head ruefully. "Oh, Tanner. You don't have to worry about that. Apparently Colette was worried about the same thing, and she and I had a long talk last night."

Tanner relaxed, hoping his little discussion with Colette had prompted her to talk some sense into his baby sister.

"Trust me, I'm in no hurry to get married. In fact, I'm not sure I'll ever want to get married," she added with a airy wave of her hands.

Tanner stared at her in horror. "What do you mean you might not get married?" What in the hell had Colette told Gina? "Well, of course you'll eventually want to get married," he said. "That's what every woman wants—a husband, a home and a family of her own."

"Don't be so old-fashioned," Gina scoffed. "Nowadays women have the freedom to pursue so many choices that the automatic choice doesn't have to be to become a wife."

Was she parroting some sort of crazy feminist beliefs that Colette had fed her the night before? Tanner wasn't sure whose neck he wanted to wring...Gina's for believing that feminist hogwash or Colette's for encouraging Gina to think that way.

Before he could say anything else, a customer walked through the front door, and Gina hurried to assist her. The store was so busy that Tanner had no opportunity to talk to Colette about what she'd said to Gina the night before.

It seemed as if every pregnant woman in a four-state area decided to shop in the boutique that day. Even when there was a brief lull in customer traffic, Colette seemed to find things to do that would take her to the opposite side of the store from where Tanner was.

If he hadn't known better, he would suspect she was avoiding him. Maybe she felt guilty about whatever nonsense she'd fed Gina the night before.

At about three a man entered the store wearing blue jeans, a work shirt and a tool belt. "Hey, Colette." He smiled warmly at her.

"Hi, Mike," she said, returning the warm smile.

"Figured I'd get in a couple of hours of work this afternoon if it's all right with you."

"It's more than all right with me," she replied.

Tanner watched as the two of them walked toward the back of the store. A moment later he heard Colette's laughter ringing out, and a tiny swell of irrational jealousy swirled through him.

"That's Mike Moore," Gina said, stepping up beside her brother. "He's doing the carpentry work on the kiddy area Colette has planned."

"It's pretty late in the day just now to start working," Tanner replied. He wasn't sure why, but he didn't like the look of the blond carpenter with the easy smile and the ability to make Colette laugh so musically.

"Mike is working here as a favor to Colette, so he puts in his hours here when he's finished with his real job."

"And what's his real job?" Tanner asked as once again Colette's laugh rang out from the back of the store. "Let me guess, he's a stand-up comedian."

Gina laughed. "No, he's a union carpenter and is working on the renovations of a building nearby. He and Colette have been friends for a while. I think he has a thing for her."

"This isn't a baby shop," Tanner muttered under his breath. "It's a swinging singles' club."

Gina laughed and moved away from him to greet a customer coming through the door. Tanner walked to the back, where Colette was explaining what she wanted to Mike.

"Two little tables…like miniature picnic tables," she said. "And I'm going to order a kit of one of those wooden fortlike structures with a slide."

"So, you really want to go with the feel of a park," Mike said.

"Exactly." Colette saw Tanner and quickly made introductions between the two men.

"So, you're just in town for a couple of days?" Mike asked him. Tanner nodded. "Have you visited Kansas City before?"

"Several times, but it's been years since the last time," Tanner replied.

"Then you should get your sister to take you on a little tour. We've got some great places to see here. There's Science City, and the River Market area and the Plaza."

"I don't think Tanner intends to be here long enough to see all the charms of our city," Colette said, not looking at Tanner.

"On the contrary," Tanner said. "I'd love to see some of the city attractions while I'm here. But I imagine Colette would be a better tour guide than Gina, who knows no more about the city than I do."

"Unfortunately, that won't be possible. I'm just too busy to take off for sight-seeing," she replied, her gaze still not meeting his. She smiled at Mike. "We'll just let you get to work now."

She didn't wait for Tanner to follow but hurried to where Gina was helping an older woman who was looking at the cribs.

Tanner walked back to the chair behind the cash register, his gaze lingering thoughtfully on Colette.

She was definitely avoiding him, and he wasn't sure if the reason was because of the kiss they'd shared or because of whatever crazy conversation she'd had with Gina the night before.

She could avoid him here, but sooner or later he was going to have a little talk with her. A renewed burst of irritation swept through him as he thought of his sister and her sudden spouting of feminism.

Tanner had nothing against feminists. He believed in equality for both sexes, understood the need for self-fulfillment. But he knew there were women who talked about personal fulfillment and the strength of women who were secretly not feminists, but something more—male bashers and man haters.

Was that what Colette was? Would she teach Gina to hate men? Would she foster in Gina a belief that women were better off without men in their lives? Would she encourage Gina to take her pleasure with men, but never commit to a real relationship that required give and take?

He thought of the kiss he and Colette had shared. She certainly hadn't kissed like a male hater. There had been a hunger in her lips, a hunger that had stirred a like response in him.

Even now, thinking about it, a surge of desire welled up inside him. He wanted to yell at her for whatever she'd said to Gina the night before, then he wanted to kiss her until they were both dizzy with desire.

But at the moment both things seemed out of the question. He couldn't help but believe she was intentionally avoiding any conversation, any contact with him whatsoever. And throughout the course of the afternoon nothing occurred to change his mind.

It wasn't until the part-time help arrived and Colette grabbed her purse to leave that Tanner saw his opportunity to speak with her alone.

When she left the store to walk home, he hurried after her and quickly fell into step next to her.

"Tanner, it really isn't necessary for you to walk me home each day that you're here in town," she said, her voice radiating a touch of irritation.

"Well, it's important that I do so now, as you've obviously been avoiding me all day and have made it impossible for me to speak to you alone," he replied, trying not to notice how the early-evening sunshine spun golden sparks into her hair.

"Don't be ridiculous, I haven't been avoiding you." The edge of vexation was more thick in her voice. "Besides, what could you possibly have to speak to me about?"

Her attitude sent a burst of irritation through him. "I'd like to know just what in the hell you told Gina last night."

She stopped walking and stared at him. "What are you talking about?" She didn't wait for his response, but rather began walking again, this time faster, as if she couldn't wait to get to her apartment and away from him.

He hurried to catch up with her. "I'm talking about

the fact that before last night Gina had always talked about getting married and having a family of her own. But suddenly after having a little late-night chat with you, she's decided she may never get married."

Once again Colette stopped and faced him, hands on her hips. "Last night you were worried she'd get serious and get married too young. Now you're worried that she'll never get married. Why don't you leave her alone and let her figure out what she wants in life by herself?"

"Because I'm afraid of what kind of influence you'll be on her."

She stared at him in surprise, opened her mouth as if to speak, then clamped it closed and stalked away. Tanner once again hurried after her. "I mean, it's not that I think you're a terrible person or anything like that," he tried to explain. "It's just that I don't know you well enough to know if your value system is up to the same standards I want Gina to embrace."

"My value system?"

She didn't stop walking, didn't speak another word to him until she reached her apartment building. It was then she turned back to face him. He'd always believed that brown eyes were warm and inviting, but hers radiated nothing close to warmth or invitation.

"You've raised Gina since she was ten," she said, the words clipped and curt. "If you think I can mess up her value system with my substandard one in a single night of conversation, then I guess maybe you didn't do such a great job raising her.''

She pulled open the door that led into the apartment building. ''And now if you'll excuse me, I have six naked dancing men waiting for me inside. I'm going to get drunk and have sex with them all because my value system doesn't tell me there's anything wrong with that.'' With these words she disappeared into the building and slammed the door.

Tanner stared after her, wondering what the hell had just happened.

Chapter Five

Colette slammed her apartment door and threw her purse down on the sofa. She had never been so insulted in her life. How dare Tanner Rothman confront her about her morals! How dare he imply that her value system was so poor she shouldn't be around his precious baby sister.

He knew nothing about her values or morals. He knew nothing about her. The man had hardly spent any time with her, certainly not enough to judge her morality. She just wished he'd take his stubborn, judgmental self back to Kansas where he could rule the world around him.

She kicked off her shoes and stalked into the kitchen, anger still driving her. She put the teakettle on, hoping a cup of tea would calm her down.

Leaning against the counter while she waited for the water to boil, she thought over the conversation with Tanner.

Now that the heat of the moment had passed, she recognized that she might have overreacted to everything he had said...might have overreacted to him.

She'd awakened that morning with the heat of his kiss from the night before still warming her lips and a desire for him to kiss her again.

It had frightened her, and she'd reacted defensively, trying to avoid him all day. She had spent most of the day trying to be in an area of her store where he was not.

Her anger with their brief discussion on the way home had been far greater than the situation warranted, but it was an anger that had made her feel safe, invulnerable to his charm and sexy attractiveness.

The teakettle whistled shrilly and she quickly made herself a cup of tea, adding an extra dollop of sugar for comfort.

Still, even though she had overreacted somewhat, it still irritated her that he somehow believed she might be a bad influence on Gina.

She knew she needed to continue to embrace her irritation...her anger where Tanner was concerned. She had a feeling it was the only thing that would keep her safe until he left to return to his ranch in Foxrun.

It was almost a relief when Gina called and told her she wouldn't be home for dinner, that Tanner was taking her out to eat and she'd be home later. Good. Perhaps the two could work things out and Tanner would go home.

At about the time she thought Tanner and Gina should be finished eating and returning to the apartment, Colette went to bed. She was still smarting from what Tanner had said to her on their way home, and she told herself she had absolutely no desire to see him.

The next morning as she left the apartment building she was vaguely surprised that he didn't show up. She got her bagels from Johnny's Café, then continued on to the shop.

Maybe he'd gone back to his ranch, she thought a few minutes later as she sipped a cup of coffee and ate a blueberry bagel. Maybe he'd given up on getting Gina to return to the ranch, had accepted defeat and left Kansas City behind.

Funny how the thought sent a tiny wave of disappointment through her. She studiously tamped the emotion away. Why should she be disappointed if she never saw Tanner Rothman again?

She certainly had no illusions of any kind about developing a relationship with him. She didn't want a relationship with any man. She would have her baby and her work, and that was enough for her.

Besides, as far as she was concerned, Tanner was

authoritarian, judgmental and self-righteous. She finished her bagel and coffee and decided to open the shop early. It was the Friday before Mother's Day and she was expecting a lot of traffic both today and tomorrow.

She opened the shop, then took a seat behind the cash register, noting with a frown that the morning was gray and held the threat of rain. She hoped the pall of the day wouldn't keep shoppers away.

By the time Gina came in at noon, lightning slashed across the city sky and thunder rumbled overhead. "It looks like it's really going to come down any minute," Gina exclaimed as she came through the door.

"Hopefully it will blow over quickly," Colette replied. No customers were in the store at the moment, and she was grateful Gina had appeared alone.

Gina stashed her purse beneath the counter, then eyed Colette curiously. "You were already in bed last night when we got back from dinner so I haven't had a chance to talk to you."

"So, where did you eat?" Colette asked curiously.

"At the Italian Gardens. The food was wonderful, but the company stank." She eyed Colette curiously. "I don't know what happened between you and Tanner when he walked you home last night, but he was a grouchy bear for the rest of the evening."

Colette decided she must secretly be a bad person, because the thought that she'd managed to make Tanner cranky somehow pleased her. "Did he give up the battle for your soul and go back home?'' she asked.

Gina laughed dryly. ''Tanner doesn't give up that easily.'' Her laughter died and she frowned thoughtfully. ''I hate to see him so upset with me. He gave up his whole life to raise me, and I feel like I'm somehow betraying him by not doing what he wants me to do.''

''I'm sure Tanner didn't take on the job of raising you believing that you would be indebted to him to the point where you would sacrifice your sense of self and all your personal dreams.''

''I know.'' Gina sighed miserably. ''I just feel so guilty about wanting things other than what he wants for me. I know he truly believes what he wants for me is best, and I don't know how to make him understand that his dreams and mine are different.''

''Have you tried just sitting down and rationally explaining it to him?'' Colette asked.

''There is no rational conversation between me and Tanner when it comes to this issue,'' she exclaimed. ''I thought maybe you could talk some sense into him, make him understand that it's time he lets me find my own way.''

''Oh, no.'' Colette held up both her hands. ''There's no way I'm going to try to talk your brother into anything. Besides, he wouldn't listen to me. He doesn't even like me.''

Gina laughed. ''Whatever gave you that idea?''

She gazed slyly at Colette. "He likes you all right. I've seen the way he looks at you, and I've never seen him look at any other woman like that."

"Then I think you must need glasses," Colette replied, her cheeks warming with the heat of a blush.

Their conversation was interrupted by a handful of women rushing in to escape the rain that had just begun to fall. The afternoon flew by, and Colette was irritated to discover that even though Tanner wasn't anywhere in the store, she couldn't get him out of her mind.

She wanted to ask Gina where he was, what he might be doing, but she knew it was none of her business and she certainly didn't want to give Gina the impression that she cared.

She didn't care. He meant nothing to her. Except that she'd loved the feel of his strong arms around her. Except that she'd loved the way his lips had taken command of her own.

It was almost time for her to go home when a taxi pulled up in front of the store and Tanner got out. He ran inside, shaking raindrops from his hair like a dog after a bath. Colette tried to ignore the way her heart leaped at the handsome sight of him.

"I thought you might have taken the day off," he said to her.

"Why would I do that?" she asked coolly.

He grinned, a teasing sexy grin that shot electricity through her veins. "I thought maybe you would have to recuperate after your wild night with the naked dancing men.''

"What naked dancing men?" Gina asked as she joined them next to the register.

"Never mind," Colette replied. "Your brother is simply attempting to be funny."

"Actually, I'm attempting in my own special clumsy fashion to apologize for what I said yesterday," he replied, his blue eyes shining earnestly. "It wasn't my intention to offend you."

"What did you do to offend her?" Gina asked, her gaze going from her brother to Colette, then back again. "What's going on?" she asked with frustration.

"None of your business, poppet," Tanner replied and touched the tip of her nose with his index finger. He looked back at Colette. "So, is my apology accepted?"

She hesitated a moment, then nodded stiffly. She wanted to stay mad at him, felt as if she needed to hang on to her anger, but it was impossible with his brilliant blue eyes appealing to her.

"Good," he said with satisfaction. "And now I have a question to ask you." He looked at Colette. "Do you have plans with your mother for Sunday?"

It always surprised Colette when thoughts of her mother sent a hollow ache radiating inside of her. When would that ache finally disappear forever? She shook her head. "Lillian is going to be out of town for the weekend," she said.

"And the shop isn't open on Mother's Day?"

"That's right. We're never open on Sundays."

"Then how about the three of us do a nice dinner together on Sunday...my treat," he suggested.

"That sounds like a great idea," Gina agreed instantly.

"It isn't necessary for you to take me out to dinner," Colette protested.

"But it is, and I insist," Tanner said, a touch of steely intent in his voice. "Why don't we plan on dining around six Sunday evening. I'll pick you ladies up at about five-thirty."

"Sounds good to me," Gina said. Colette merely nodded.

"Oh, and since it was close to the time you went home yesterday, I told the taxi to wait and take you home," he said to Colette. He flashed her a charming smile. "I didn't want you to have to walk home in the rain."

"You don't have to take care of me," she replied. "I'm perfectly capable of taking care of myself."

She wanted to be irritated by his arranging for the taxi.

She didn't need or want anyone to take care of her. But someplace deep inside she was also touched by the gesture.

Aware that she had sounded less than gracious, she

continued. "But thank you for your thoughtfulness. I guess I'll head home right now."

Moments later, ensconced in the back of the taxi with the driving rain beating against the windows, she thought of the dinner invitation for Sunday.

She told herself there was absolutely nothing wrong with her having dinner with Tanner and his sister. It wasn't as if she was going to be spending any time alone with Tanner. There would be no opportunity for him to kiss her again, which was just fine with her.

She tried to imagine what Tanner's reaction would be if he knew she'd been artificially inseminated and intended to raise a child alone. There was no doubt in her mind that he would heartily disapprove.

Of course, there was no reason for her to tell him of her future plans. And she certainly didn't need or want his blessing on the choices she made in her life.

"Hey, lady, you gonna sit back there and wait for the rain to stop, or are you getting out?" The cabby eyed her in the rearview mirror, his voice pulling Colette from her thoughts.

"I'm getting out," she exclaimed. She opened her purse, withdrew money and leaned over the seat to pay him, but he waved her away.

"The gentleman already took care of it," he said.

Colette jumped out of the cab and raced through the rain for her apartment door, wondering why, in spite of all her reservations about Tanner, a rush of anticipation filled her as she thought of dinner on Sunday night.

Tanner checked his reflection in the dresser mirror one last time. The slacks and dress shirt he'd bought the day before fit nicely and were a pleasant change from the jeans and T-shirts he normally wore.

He'd told himself he'd bought the new clothes in honor of the mother he'd lost eleven years before, but as he'd picked out the shirt, he'd found himself wondering what Colette's favorite colors were. Did she like pullover shirts or buttons?

Colette. He'd insulted her the other night with his concern about her morals and values. He hadn't meant to, but that had been the end result.

Friday at the shop she'd accepted his apology, but he had a feeling she'd accepted it grudgingly. He hoped that over dinner this evening he could somehow make amends for his thoughtlessness.

Looking at his watch, he realized it was time for him to leave. He splashed cologne around his neck, raked a hand through his hair, then left the hotel room.

He'd arranged for one of the hotel cars and drivers to be at his disposal for the evening, and when he stepped out of the hotel door, the car was awaiting him.

He hadn't gone to the shop yesterday, had spent part of the day on the phone with his foreman making sure things were running smoothly at the ranch. Then, in the afternoon, he'd gone on a hunt for a special restaurant for their Mother's Day celebration dinner.

He'd found the perfect place not far from his hotel. Antonio's was elegant, with tables arranged to provide maximum seclusion and privacy for diners. The menu offered a variety of choices and the wine list was extensive. He'd made reservations, then gone hunting for appropriate clothes for a special dinner.

There was only one thing he wished could happen that night—he wished that his mother could be present. He rarely allowed himself to think of his parents. The loss still hurt after all these years.

But today when the hotel restaurant had been filled with families and mothers wearing corsages and smiles, it had been difficult to get his mother out of his mind. If she'd been able to attend the dinner this evening, he would have bought her a corsage of baby pink roses, her favorite.

The driver pulled up in front of Colette's apartment building, and Tanner shoved thoughts of his mother from his mind. "I'll be right back," he told the driver, who nodded.

A few moments later Tanner knocked on Gina and Colette's apartment door. Colette answered, and for a moment as Tanner gazed at her, he found speech next to impossible.

Unlike the tailored suits she wore to work, the caramel-colored dress she now wore clung to her breasts and slender waist, then flared out in softly feminine folds to her knees.

The V-neckline of the dress was just low enough to be interesting without being overtly distracting, and her brown eyes were the same lovely color as the material.

Her cheeks turned a pretty pink.

"I'm sorry, I'm staring, aren't I?"

"Yes, you are," she replied.

"You deserve to be stared at. You look terrific," he said as she gestured him inside.

"Thanks. You don't look so bad yourself," she replied, her cheeks still brightly colored.

"Are we ready to go? I hope you're hungry."

"Starving," she replied. "And I'm ready, but Gina is still in her room."

Tanner looked at his watch, then back to her. "I have reservations at Antonio's. Have you ever been there?"

"No, although I've heard it's wonderful." She toyed with the strap of her purse, obviously ill at ease. Her gaze darted everywhere around the room but at him.

He shifted from foot to foot, unsure how to put her at ease when he wasn't sure why she appeared so uncomfortable. "It's a beautiful evening," he finally said.

"Yes," she agreed. "There's nothing nicer than spring evenings." She finally looked at him and offered him a smile that caused the dimple to dance provocatively in her left cheek. "Unless it's autumn evenings."

"Autumn is nice," he agreed, wondering how long they could keep a conversation about the weather flowing.

A knock fell on the door. She frowned. "I wonder who that could be." She hurried to the door and opened it.

Danny stepped into the living room. "Hi, Colette...Mr. Rothman."

Tanner looked at the young man in confusion. Had Gina invited him to join them and neglected to tell Tanner? At that moment Gina came out of the bedroom.

She looked like a ray of sunshine in a bright yellow dress that enhanced her dark-haired prettiness. A burst of love swept through Tanner. "Is Danny joining us for dinner?" he asked her.

Gina looked at him in surprise. "Didn't I tell you?"

"Tell me what?" Tanner asked.

"Danny invited me to have dinner with him and his parents at their house. I thought I told you." She gave Tanner a look of innocence, one that he didn't buy for a minute. He wondered if she hadn't told him of her change in plans because she was afraid he'd be angry.

"Is there a problem, sir?" Danny asked hesitantly. "I can call my parents and let them know there's been a change of plans."

"No...no problem," Tanner replied, and shot his

sister a look he knew she would understand that meant they would talk later.

"Then I'm all ready." Gina smiled. "You two have a wonderful time. I know we're going to." She linked her arm through Danny's, and with murmured goodbyes, they flew out the door.

"Well, that was a surprise," Tanner said as he turned back to Colette. "You ready to go?"

"Oh, Tanner, it isn't necessary that you take me to dinner," she protested, and set her purse down in the nearby chair.

He walked over, picked up her purse and held it out to her. "On the contrary. I haven't eaten all day in anticipation of savoring Antonio's fare, and I had to grease the palm of the maître d' in order to assure our reservation."

Still he sensed her hesitation. "Please, Colette," he said. "Have dinner with me. There's nothing I hate more than eating alone."

"All right," she finally relented, then smiled teasingly. "But only because it's Antonio's and I've always wanted to eat there." She took her purse from him and together they left the apartment.

As he escorted her to the waiting car, he wondered why he wasn't angry at Gina. The second thing he wondered about was why he was oddly pleased that it was just going to be him and Colette for the evening.

Chapter Six

The back seat of the car was too small. However, Colette had a feeling even the back seat of a stretch limo would be too small if she was sharing the confines with Tanner.

His thigh pressed warmly against hers, and the scent of his cologne filled her senses. She hadn't bargained for dinner alone with Tanner. She'd wanted—needed—Gina to be here, as well.

He looked more handsome than she'd ever seen him. Gone were the jeans and T-shirts he'd worn since arriving in Kansas City. The navy slacks fit him as if tailor-made for his long legs, and the blue-and-dark-gray-striped shirt clung to his broad shoulders, yet tapered in at his slender waist.

She gripped her purse tightly in her lap, trying to

make herself as small as possible so there would be less physical contact between them.

"I'm trying to figure out why Gina didn't tell me about her plans with Danny and his family," he said, breaking the silence that had grown uncomfortable between them.

"Maybe she didn't want you to throw a fit," Colette replied.

"I don't throw fits," he replied defensively. She eyed him in disbelief. "I'm not some kind of ogre," he added. "I'm just a concerned big brother who is misunderstood." His eyes twinkled with a teasing light.

"Misunderstood, my foot," Colette replied dryly.

Again the silence resumed between them. Colette stared out the passenger window, trying to ignore the electric currents that seemed to pass from his warm muscular thigh to hers.

"You know, I really don't want to keep Gina from seeking her own future," he finally said. "I only wish she'd postpone it for a year. I'd like to see her finish college, then I would support her wholeheartedly in whatever she chose to do." He turned to Colette and smiled. "And that's the last thing I intend to say on the subject for the remainder of the evening."

Again an uncomfortable silence sprang up between them. Colette folded and unfolded the strap of her purse, desperately trying to ignore his closeness.

GET FREE BOOKS and a FREE GIFT WHEN YOU PLAY THE...

SLOT MACHINE GAME!

Just scratch off the silver box with a coin. Then check below to see the gifts you get!

YES! I have scratched off the silver box. Please send me the 2 free Silhouette Romance® books and gift for which I qualify. I understand I am under no obligation to purchase any books, as explained on the back of this card.

315 SDL DRRE

215 SDL DRRU
(S-R-02/03)

FIRST NAME

LAST NAME

ADDRESS

APT.#

CITY

STATE/PROV.

ZIP/POSTAL CODE

7	7	7
🍒	🍒	🍒
♣	♣	♣
🔔	🔔	🍒

Worth TWO FREE BOOKS plus a BONUS Mystery Gift!

Worth TWO FREE BOOKS!

Worth ONE FREE BOOK!

TRY AGAIN!

Visit us online at www.eHarlequin.com

Offer limited to one per household and not valid to current Silhouette Romance® subscribers. All orders subject to approval.

© 2000 HARLEQUIN ENTERPRISES LTD. ® and TM are trademarks owned by Harlequin Books S.A. used under license.

The Silhouette Reader Service™ — Here's how it works:

Accepting your 2 free books and gift places you under no obligation to buy anything. You may keep the books and gift and return the shipping statement marked "cancel." If you do not cancel, about a month later we'll send you 6 additional books and bill you just $3.34 each in the U.S., or $3.80 each in Canada, plus 25¢ shipping & handling per book and applicable taxes if any.* That's the complete price and — compared to cover prices of $3.99 each in the U.S. and $4.50 each in Canada — it's quite a bargain! You may cancel at any time, but if you choose to continue, every month we'll send you 6 more books, which you may either purchase at the discount price or return to us and cancel your subscription.

*Terms and prices subject to change without notice. Sales tax applicable in N.Y. Canadian residents will be charged applicable provincial taxes and GST.

If offer card is missing write to: Silhouette Reader Service, 3010 Walden Ave., P.O. Box 1867, Buffalo NY 14240-1867

BUSINESS REPLY MAIL

FIRST-CLASS MAIL   PERMIT NO. 717-003   BUFFALO, NY

POSTAGE WILL BE PAID BY ADDRESSEE

SILHOUETTE READER SERVICE
3010 WALDEN AVE
PO BOX 1867
BUFFALO NY 14240-9952

NO POSTAGE
NECESSARY
IF MAILED
IN THE
UNITED STATES

"So, how'd you spend your day off today?" he asked.

"I slept sinfully late, then went to my mother's place to take care of her neurotic little poodle, since Lillian and her latest boyfriend are out of town."

"I take it that you don't like dogs," he asked.

"I like dogs just fine," she replied. "But Cuddles is the most yapping, biting, whining dog I've ever met."

A tremendous sense of relief flooded through her as they pulled up outside of the restaurant and got out of the car.

She couldn't help but be slightly impressed when the maître d' greeted him by name. "Ah, Mr. Rothman, you're right on time and we have your table waiting for you."

"You must have greased his palm very well," Colette murmured as they followed him through the elegant restaurant.

Tanner grinned. As they walked, he placed a hand in the small of her back, and the heat of his touch seemed to radiate through her from head to toe.

The maître d' led them to a small table in the back of the restaurant. With latticework and thick, hanging greenery on three sides, the table was secluded and lit with a single candle in the center.

"It will just be the two of us," Tanner said as the man pulled out a chair for Colette. The table held three place settings.

"Very well." The maître d' motioned a bus boy over and he quickly whisked the extra place setting from the table. "Your server will be with you momentarily," the maître d' said, then scurried away, leaving Tanner and Colette alone.

"Very nice," Colette said, looking around. She was beginning to relax somewhat, now that she was seated a comfortable distance across the table from Tanner and the scent in her nose was wonderful cooking smells rather than the evocative fragrance of him.

"It is nice, isn't it," he agreed.

She smiled. "I'll bet Foxrun doesn't have restaurants like this."

He leaned back in his chair and returned her smile. "True, but the restaurants in Foxrun have their own brand of charm."

She picked up her water glass and took a sip, trying not to note how the candlelight sparked attractive silvery glints in his deep blue eyes. "And what are the charms of the restaurants in Foxrun?"

"They're kind of like that bar on the sitcom where everyone knows your name. Every Thursday at Millie's Family Restaurant, Millie bakes a caramel apple pie because she knows I eat there on Thursdays."

"And you like caramel apple pies?"

He grinned. "It's my favorite. My mother used to bake caramel apple pies for me." His grin faltered and he picked up his napkin and spread it on his lap.

At that moment the waitress appeared at their table.

"Can I get you something to drink before I take your orders?" she asked.

"Nothing for me," Colette said.

"Are you sure? How about a glass of wine?" Tanner asked.

She shook her head. "No, thank you." She pointed to her water glass. "I'm fine."

"I'd like a Scotch on the rocks," he said to the waitress.

Colette was grateful he hadn't pushed the issue. While she would have loved to enjoy a glass of wine, she was also mindful of the fact that she might at this very moment be pregnant.

The waitress brought Tanner his drink, then they placed their orders and she once again departed from the table. Tanner looked out to the other diners in their view and for a moment Colette drank in his handsome features.

There was little hint of the rancher in him this evening. In his well-fitting dress clothes, he could have been anything. A banker, a businessman, a stockbroker, but one thing was for sure, he wore the self-confidence of a successful man like a mantle around his shoulders.

However, as he gazed out at the other diners in his view, she thought she saw a hint of sadness in his eyes. "This must be a difficult day for you," she said.

He looked at her and smiled. "In some ways it is,"

he agreed. "As I see families celebrating with their mothers, I can't help but miss mine just a little."

"Tell me about her," Colette prompted, suddenly interested to learn about the woman who had raised him.

The softness that tempered his features was overwhelmingly appealing. He took a sip of his Scotch, then set the glass back on the table and turned it between his big hands.

"Her name was Mariah and I thought she was the prettiest woman in the entire world. She always smelled good and she smiled and sang almost all the time. She loved pink roses and had a huge garden of them on the south side of the house. Whenever there was a southern breeze, she'd opened the window and the entire house would smell of the flowers' scents."

"Sounds nice."

"She was nice...and I wasn't the only one who thought she was beautiful. She was one of the first Miss Dairy Cows."

"Miss Dairy Cow?" Colette eyed him curiously. "What exactly is a Miss Dairy Cow?"

"Once a year Foxrun holds a big fair, and a young woman is chosen Miss Dairy Cow and represents the county at a variety of functions over the course of the year. Gina was Miss Dairy Cow last year." Tanner grinned. "I know it sounds pretty corny, but it's all in good fun."

"I think it sounds wonderful," Colette replied. "Did your mother work?"

"She worked hard at being a homemaker," he replied.

"So she was a traditional kind of woman." Somehow Colette wasn't surprised by this information. She would have guessed traditional, conservative parents had raised Tanner.

"Definitely traditional." He took another sip of his drink and stared down into the amber liquid, as if all his memories of his mother were retained there. "She truly loved taking care of us...cooking favorite meals, decorating the house with fresh flowers and things that transformed it into a home."

"So she didn't work outside the home?" Colette asked.

"No." He smiled, the teasing glint back in his eyes. "Apparently, she was fulfilled as a woman just being a wife and a mother."

"Ah, so that explains it," she exclaimed.

One of his dark brows quirked upward. "Explains what?"

"That explains why you hate women who work. I suppose you're one of those Neanderthals who believe in keeping a wife barefoot and pregnant."

He leaned forward, and despite the odors of food that filled the air, she could smell his scent, as well. It was that refreshingly clean, slightly spiced fragrance that she found wonderfully appealing.

"Not really, but I am one of those who will believe in practicing frequently to get my wife pregnant." His voice was smooth and low, and Colette felt it in the pit of her stomach as if she'd just swigged a shot of his Scotch.

He leaned back once again and gazed at her in amusement. "Of course, that is if I ever decide to take a wife," he added.

This man with his devilishly sexy eyes and deep, hypnotic voice could make an ice cube in the Antarctic melt, Colette thought. At that moment the waitress arrived with their salads and a basket of yeasty rolls.

"Tell me about Lillian," he said once the waitress had again departed. "You mentioned the other day you thought she would have been happy had you moved out at six years old. What did you mean by that?"

Colette stabbed a cherry tomato with her fork and thought of her mother. "Unlike your mom, Lillian took little pleasure in parenting or creating a home."

How many times had Colette heard the words, "run along," "get away," "don't hang on me." "She was either out or busy or sleeping most of the time when I was growing up." She popped the tomato into her mouth and chewed.

"Did she work outside the home?"

She nodded. "Yes, but never at one place for too

long. She always made the mistake of mixing business with pleasure. She'd start dating a co-worker or her boss, then the romance would end and she'd be devastated and have to quit the job." She moved a piece of purple onion from one side of her salad to the other. "I've always felt just a little bit sorry for her," she continued.

"Why?"

She set her fork down, then looked up and met Tanner's gaze. "She's always had a sort of desperation when it came to men. It's like if she isn't part of a man's life, her own life disappears entirely. When she wasn't dating anyone she'd spend days in bed, too depressed to get up."

Tanner reached across the table and covered her hand with his. "That must have been tough on you. Kids want to believe that they are the priority in their parents' lives."

Not as tough as feeling his warm gaze on her and his slightly callused hand covering hers. She shrugged and pulled her hand from his. "Don't get me wrong, my childhood wasn't awful. I wasn't beaten or abused."

She picked up her fork once again, uncomfortable by the softness in his eyes. "Enough about me," she said. "Tell me more about your childhood. What was your father like?"

She didn't want to think about Lillian any longer,

and more than anything she wanted Tanner to stop looking at her in the way that created a ball of warmth in the pit of her stomach.

Tanner leaned back in his chair once again. The little she'd shared with him about her mother had touched him deeply. More than that, what he sensed had been left unspoken touched him even more deeply.

What she hadn't spoken of was the deep loneliness of a neglected child, but he had heard it echoing in her voice. Her brown eyes had radiated pain despite the fact that she hadn't spoken of any hurt.

And what amazed him more than anything was that for just a moment he'd wanted to stand up and pull her into his arms, somehow try to ease the ache he sensed inside of her.

"My dad was sort of quiet," he said in answer to her question. "He worked long hours at the ranch and didn't play as big a role in mine and Gina's lives as my mother did, but he was a good man, who adored my mother and loved us."

"They certainly must have done something right," she said. "It isn't every twenty-one-year-old young man who would step up to the plate and accept the responsibilities you did with Gina."

He shrugged and took another sip of his Scotch. "There was never any question about stepping up to the plate," he replied. "We had no other family, no aunts or uncles who could take in Gina, and I certainly wasn't going to see her in foster care. The minute I got the call about my parents' deaths, I packed up my bags and returned home immediately.''

''Returned home?''

He nodded. ''I was in Lawrence at the time, in my junior year at Kansas University.'' He grinned at her. ''Don't look at me that way,'' he said. ''I know that you're thinking it's important to me that Gina finish her schooling because I'm somehow living my youth vicariously through her.''

She smiled, flashing her enchanting dimple. ''That's exactly what I was thinking.''

''But it isn't true.'' He stopped talking as the waitress appeared to take away their salad plates and serve them their entrees.

He continued once they were alone again. ''I'm not living my youth vicariously through Gina, because I don't feel like I lost any of my youth. I don't feel like I sacrificed anything by leaving school and taking care of her and the ranch.'' He shrugged. ''College had been my parents' idea. I'd always wanted just to work at the ranch.''

''Then why can't you accept that Gina might be satisfied working as a salesclerk?''

''I can accept that,'' he replied as he picked up his fork and knife in preparation for cutting the thick, juicy steak on his plate. ''But if she finishes college and has her degree, she has something else to fall back on later if she changes her mind about sales.''

He smiled. "But I thought we'd decided we weren't going to talk about Gina this evening."

"You're absolutely right," she agreed.

For the next few minutes they focused on their meal, talking about how wonderful everything tasted. "Do you cook?" he asked.

She grinned, and again he was struck by her prettiness and tried to keep his gaze away from the teasing neckline of her dress that offered him a view of the swell of her creamy breasts.

"I'll bet you think I'm going to say no," she said, her eyes sparkling like chunks of topaz. "I'll bet you think I do nothing but buy junk- and convenience-food. But the truth is that I started cooking at a very early age and discovered I loved it. I just don't have the time to cook or bake much these days." She cut off a piece of her chicken cordon bleu. "What about you? Are you a good cook?"

"I know more dishes made with macaroni and cheese than anyone on this earth," he replied.

She laughed, the melodic sound shooting warmth through him. "I take it from that comment that cooking is not your strong suit."

"No." He gazed at her intently. "But there are other things I consider myself to be very good at. Would you like to find out what they are?"

He was rewarded by the slight reddening of her cheeks. "Why, Mr. Rothman, are you attempting to flirt with me?"

"Maybe," he replied, delighting in the deepening color of her blush. He recognized that he'd been on a slow simmer from the moment she'd opened the door of her apartment.

He couldn't help but notice that the candle glow loved her features. It illuminated her beautiful eyes and warmed her touchable skin, heightening his simmer to something more intense.

"Why would you want to flirt with me?" she asked, averting her gaze from his.

"Why wouldn't I?" She looked at him and he once again leaned forward and reached out and lightly stroked the back of her hand. "You're a very attractive woman, and I'm a normal, healthy man who finds you very desirable."

"That's ridiculous," she exclaimed and quickly pulled her hand from his. "You don't really know me. I'm not even sure you like me." Her voice was slightly breathless, letting him know she wasn't immune to his touch.

"What does that have to do with wanting you?" He laughed at her look of outrage. "Just kidding," he replied. He picked up his fork once again, still gazing at her. "You're right, I don't know you very well. But I never said I didn't like you."

"Well, there's no point in you flirting with me," she said.

"Why not?"

"Because I don't have meaningless affairs, and

you'll be returning soon to Foxrun.'' She looked at
him, a touch of defiance in her beautiful eyes. "And
although I don't know you very well, I'm not at all
sure that I like you.''

Tanner laughed, surprised at the burst of energy her
words provoked in him. He couldn't remember the
last time a woman had challenged him. "Then, we'll
just have to see if I can change that.''

"Don't count on it,'' she said dryly.

He grinned at her. "So, tell me about all your old
boyfriends.''

"Don't be silly. One of the first rules women learn
is that when you're with one man, you don't talk
about other men,'' she exclaimed.

"Really. And who teaches that rule?''

"It's in the rule book all women are handed at
birth.''

He laughed and for the next few minutes they
spoke about people they had dated in the past. Tanner
told her about the girl he'd dated in college, a young
woman named Sally whom he'd thought he'd eventually marry.

But when Sally learned that he was going to raise
his sister, she'd suddenly lost interest in him. He also
confessed that there had been few women after Sally,
that raising Gina had been a full-time job.

"Other than the naked dancing men, there have
been few men in my past,'' she said, making him
laugh.

"Why?" he asked when he'd sobered.

She shrugged, the movement giving him a tantalizing view of the curve of her breasts. "From the time I was fifteen years old, I was working two jobs, saving every dime for the day when I could open my own shop. Between school and work there was never enough time for dating."

He realized Colette was a woman who had never been taken care of. From what she'd told him about her mother, about her life, she'd always had to take care of herself. He thought of her working two jobs at such a young age, and his desire for her was tempered with a soft tenderness.

"What about Mike?" he asked. "The guy who's doing your carpentry work at the shop. Gina thinks there's a possibility of something going on between you and him."

She threw back her head and laughed. "Gina is at that age where she sees romance everywhere. Mike and I are just friends. He's had the same girlfriend for as long as I've known him, and she just had his baby last month. He's doing the work for me in exchange for store credit."

Tanner was surprised at the relief that flooded through him. Why should he care whether Colette had a thing for the handsome carpenter working for her? It wasn't as if Tanner intended to have a relationship with Colette.

They finished the meal discussing more banal topics—the weather, the tourist attractions in Kansas City, the latest tattoo craze that had swept the country.

"I thought about getting a tattoo once," she shocked Tanner by saying. "I was going to get a butterfly on my ankle."

"What changed your mind?"

She daintily dabbed her napkin to her mouth, then returned it back to her lap. "Besides the fact that I'm really not into self-inflicted pain, I decided I didn't want to spend the money."

"Money is important to you," he observed. He thought he knew what her answer would be. She was a cool, calculating businesswoman, and money had to be what drove her.

She took a sip of her water and cocked her head, her brow wrinkled in thought. "Yes and no," she surprised him by saying. "Certainly money is important in that I want to be able to pay my rent and buy groceries and pay bills. But it's all about more than money."

She paused a moment and took another sip of her water, then smiled a sad little smile that touched Tanner's heart. "I grew up listening to my mother tell me I'd probably never amount to anything. Whenever Lillian was unhappy with her own life, she said hurtful things to me. Instead of getting upset, I grew more determined to be successful, to get myself in a position where I never had to depend on or need anyone other than myself."

"Needing others isn't necessarily a bad thing," Tanner protested, surprised to find himself disturbed by her words.

At that moment their waitress arrived to ask if either of them would care for dessert. "Not for me," Colette said. "I couldn't eat another bite."

"Me, neither," he agreed. The waitress slid his bill on the table, then departed. "Are you ready?" he asked.

Colette nodded and placed her napkin on the table. Tanner paid the bill, then together he and Colette left the restaurant.

As the driver took them back to her apartment building, Tanner found himself thinking about everything he had discovered about Colette over the meal.

She was softer than he'd initially believed. In talking a little bit about her mother and her past, she'd banished the picture he'd had of her as a cold, hard businesswoman without a heart.

Although she talked like a woman who was strong and independent, there had been moments when vulnerability had shone from her eyes, trembled slightly at her lips.

"Thank you, Tanner," she said as the driver pulled up in front of her building. "It was a lovely dinner."

He didn't want the night to end. He wasn't ready to part from her yet. They got out of the car, and he walked with her to the door. "It's early still. Aren't you going to invite me up for coffee?"

He saw indecision flicker in her eyes. "I don't know...." She looked at her wristwatch.

"Just a quick cup," he said. "I promise I won't stay long."

She hesitated another moment, then nodded her assent. "All right. A quick cup of coffee."

And maybe a kiss or two, Tanner thought to himself as he followed her inside. He'd never met a woman whom he sensed needed to be kissed more than Colette Carson.

Chapter Seven

Colette had not wanted to invite him inside. But after the lovely meal they'd just shared, she couldn't deny him a quick cup of coffee.

As they rode up in the elevator together, she again felt slightly overwhelmed by his nearness. She felt his gaze on her but kept her own focused on the elevator indicator that showed the floors they passed.

When the elevator stopped and the doors whooshed open, he placed his hand in the small of her back. She felt the heat of his casual touch through the material of her dress, burning through the thin silk slip and panty hose.

She breathed a sigh of relief when they reached her door and he dropped his hand from her back. She pulled out her keys and started to unlock the door.

"Allow me," he said, and smoothly took the keys from her grasp.

"What a gentleman," she said, trying to tease him to defuse the tension that bubbled inside of her.

"There are times it pays to be a gentleman, and times it pays to be a rascal." His eyes sparked with a wicked glint that heightened the tension inside her.

A quick cup of coffee, she reminded herself. Just because she and Tanner would be alone in the apartment didn't mean they were going to do anything other than chat a bit and drink coffee.

But there was that look in his eyes that made a shiver race up her spine. There was a hunger there that called on a hunger inside her.

He opened the door, then handed her back her keys. "After you," he said.

She stepped inside, dropped her purse on one of the chairs, then motioned him toward the sofa. "Why don't you just have a seat, and I'll go make the coffee."

She started to walk toward the kitchen but gasped in surprise as he grabbed her wrist and halted her forward motion.

"I've changed my mind about the coffee," he said, not releasing his hold on her. With his fingers still encircling her wrist, he stepped closer to her.

Her mouth grew dry and her heart pounded so loudly she vaguely wondered if he could hear it. "Would you rather have iced tea?" she asked. "Or lemonade. I could make a pitcher of lemonade.'' She was rambling but couldn't seem to stop herself. "Of course, not everyone likes lemonade, but it's nice and refreshing on a hot summer day."

He smiled, that bold, sexy grin that made her knees grow weak and created a flutter in the pit of her stomach. "I don't want coffee." He dropped her hand and instead wrapped his arms around her waist. "I don't want iced tea." His voice was deep, his breath warm on her face, hinting of the Scotch he'd drunk earlier in the evening.

He stroked his hands up and down her back. "I don't want lemonade," he continued. His eyes were like the blue flames of a gas stove—hot and intense. "I just want you."

"But you said you'd come in for coffee." Her voice trembled. "A gentleman doesn't enter a woman's apartment under false pretenses."

"I'm feeling more like a rascal than a gentleman."

He gave her no time to protest or deny, but claimed her lips with his.

This was exactly what Colette had been afraid of. She had been unable to get the first kiss they had shared out of her head, and as he pulled her more tightly against him, she recognized she didn't have the strength to deny him, or herself, the pleasure of this second kiss.

His mouth didn't just kiss hers but rather took full possession. At first it was just a meeting of mouths, then his tongue swirled against hers, evoking in her a warmth that was delicious.

It wasn't just the kiss that made her feel as if she'd swallowed a glowing sun. It was the pleasure of the evening they'd just shared.

She hadn't wanted to like Tanner, she'd wanted to believe he was arrogant and dictatorial and had no redeeming qualities whatsoever. But he had just enough arrogance to be attractive, and she suspected he truly was a bit dictatorial but was driven by love and caring.

As his hands once again swept up and down her back, any thoughts of Tanner's good qualities or bad qualities were lost beneath his sensual onslaught.

She felt as if she were drowning in his kiss, melting in his arms. She knew somewhere in the back of her mind that she should stop this madness. There was no future here.

But it was this thought that kept her in his arms. She knew there was no future with Tanner, that this could only be a momentary pleasure at best. So why not indulge herself?

She didn't want a man in her life permanently. She had her life carefully mapped out before her, and no-where did it include a man. But she just wanted this man for this moment in time.

"Colette...sweet Colette," he said as he broke the kiss and his mouth trailed down the length of her neck. "Since I kissed you the other night, I've thought of nothing else but kissing you again."

"I've thought about it a lot, too," she admitted, breathless from the sensation of his lips on the sensitive skin of her throat. She tilted her head back slightly to give him better access to her neck.

"I've thought about other things besides kissing you," he said, the confession pulling a renewed burst of flames through her.

"So have I," she replied.

She had no opportunity to say anything more as his mouth once again found hers, plying her lips with sweet heat that stole through her entire body.

He held her so close her breasts snuggled against his broad chest and her thighs were pressed against his.

His hands moved down and cupped her buttocks, the intimacy sending a shiver of white-hot desire through her.

She knew he wanted her…the evidence of that was apparent by their physical closeness. And she wanted him. She knew all the reasons why she shouldn't… but she did.

Still kissing her, he maneuvered them closer to the sofa, and she could feel his heartbeat banging against her own. The knowledge that she stirred him enriched the desire that flowed through her.

He moved his hands, up, up, to the back of her dress where the zipper began. Colette held her breath as she heard the hiss of the zipper falling to just below her hips, felt the cool air that indicated the dress now gaped wide open in the back.

He broke the kiss as he slid the dress from her shoulders. She caught it at her breasts, unsure how far she wanted this moment to go.

However, as she gazed into his midnight-blue eyes, she saw not only a ravenous hunger, but also a sweet tenderness, a wealth of gentleness that filled up empty places she hadn't known existed inside her.

Drawing a deep breath, she allowed the dress to fall to the floor, leaving her in her beige lace slip, her lacy white bra and her panty hose and panties. She stepped out of the pool of caramel-colored material, her heartbeat pounding so loudly in her ears she could hear nothing else.

She started for the sofa, then realized Gina could return home at any time and instead picked up her dress and walked on trembling legs to her bedroom door.

"Colette?" His voice held the sexual want that tingled in every nerve in her body.

She knew he was giving her an opportunity to change her mind, that the moment they crossed the threshold into her bedroom, there would be no turning back. But she didn't want to turn back.

With hands that trembled as violently as her legs, she opened the door and stepped into her room, grateful she'd cleaned that day and the burgundy-and-green spread was neatly made over the double bed.

Tanner followed right behind her. When he reached for the light switch, she halted him. Moonlight streamed into the window, making any artificial light unnecessary.

"You are so beautiful," Tanner whispered softly as he once again gathered her into his arms. His hands splayed across her bare shoulders as he crushed her to him.

She pulled away from him enough so she could get her hands between them. She fumbled at his shirt buttons, wanting to feel his warm expanse of broad chest beneath her fingertips.

He helped her, starting at the bottom of his shirt while she worked down from the top. When the buttons were all unfastened, he pulled it off, then swept her up in his arms and set her on the bed.

He joined her there, murmuring sweet, nonsensical words as he gathered her into his arms. When he crashed his lips back to hers, she opened her mouth eagerly. She was lost...lost to his kiss, the warmth of his skin, the slightly rough touch of his callused hands.

It didn't matter that there was no future with him. She wasn't interested in the future. She wanted only now with him. She could live the rest of her life just fine alone.

* * *

Tanner had never felt skin so smooth, so silky, and he loved the sweet, gasping sounds Colette made as he stroked down her throat, over her collarbones and across the top of her lace-covered breasts.

Her hands gripped his back as he continued his exploration of her skin, nipping at her neck with his mouth and raking his fingers across the provocative swell of her breasts.

He was enflamed with his need for her, the need to take complete possession of her body, mind and soul. With the moonlight streaking in the window, her features were bathed in a silvery glow, transforming her into a beauty that touched him to his core.

Her eyes were glazed enough that he knew she was no longer thinking, but had gone to that place where the world was made of nothing but physical sensation.

He knew that if he removed her slip, took off her bra and feasted on her naked breasts, he would be lost to that same place.

But for some reason he couldn't get out of his mind her statement that she didn't have meaningless affairs. Wasn't that just what they would be doing if he made love to her now? Indulging in a meaningless affair that he knew she would regret the moment they were finished.

He tried to shut off the loud voice of his irritating conscience, fought to get past it and lose himself in her completely. But he couldn't.

With this realization, despite his desire to the contrary, his passion ebbed. As crazy as it sounded, he liked Colette far too well to make love to her.

"Colette."

He whispered her name softly, then stroked a finger down the side of her face. She turned her cheek toward his touch, like a cat seeking a gentle caress.

"If we keep this up, you're going to hate me in the morning," he said.

The glaze that had darkened her eyes faded and she looked at him uncertainly. "Wha-what?"

He smiled, hoping that in calling a halt to their lovemaking he wasn't hurting her more than if they'd continued.

He took one of her hands in his and pulled her up to a sitting position. "As much as I'd love to make love to you, I'm not at all sure that this is the best thing for us to do."

Even in the silvery shadows of the room, he could see the fiery blush that stole over her features. "I...I can't imagine what I was thinking," she exclaimed. She scrambled off the bed and grabbed her dress.

"Darlin', there's nothing to be embarrassed about. We both just got a little carried away, that's all," he said as he also got off the bed.

"I can't imagine what possessed me," she muttered as she stepped into her dress and pulled it up. Her cheeks were still a gorgeous scarlet as she raked a hand through her short curly hair and refused to look at him.

"I was certainly doing my damnedest to possess you," he said teasingly. No responding smile curved her lips.

He walked over to her and placed his hands on her shoulders, forcing her to look at him. "I know this is awkward, Colette," he said gently. "But I figured it would be more awkward if things continued."

"You're absolutely right," she replied. "Thank you for returning me to my senses."

He smiled at her and reached behind her to pull up her dress zipper. "I'd like to say it was my pleasure, but my pleasure would have been better satisfied if my conscience hadn't kicked in."

He dropped his arms from around her and picked up his shirt from the floor. "And now I really would love a cup of coffee."

He could tell that she'd much prefer he exit her apartment as soon as possible. But he had a feeling if he left immediately, for as long as he was in town this night would stand between them. "I promise, a quick cup of coffee and I'll get out of here."

She nodded and together they left her bedroom and went into the kitchen. Tanner sat at the table while she fixed the coffee, an uncomfortable silence growing between them.

When the fragrant brew had begun to fill the glass carafe, she turned to face him. "I don't suppose you would believe me if I said I normally don't do things like this." Her gaze didn't quite meet his.

"I believe that, Colette." And he was surprised to realize he did believe it. In the space of the past few days he'd come to recognize that Colette wasn't the wild city girl he'd feared she might be.

She turned back toward the cabinets and pulled down two cups and saucers. His hunger for her reared up again and he was almost sorry the gentleman streak had kicked in.

But the moment had been lost and all she was offering him now was a cup of fresh-brewed coffee. She didn't look at him as she placed his cup before him, then sat at the opposite end of the table with her own cup.

He frowned, unsure how to break the shell of tension that had descended around them. He wanted to see her smile again, wanted to see the flash of her delightful dimple in her cheek. He wanted anything but the tense silence that had grown between them.

"I've suffered worse embarrassment than this," he finally said.

She looked at him, a spark of curiosity in her eyes. "What?" She picked up her coffee cup and took a sip.

"Jenny Marie Malcom was the prettiest girl in the sixth grade and I had a horrible crush on her. One day at lunch she was talking about how she thought bullfighters were so cool, so I invited her out to our ranch one afternoon and decided to fight the bull we had."

Colette set her cup down, her eyes sparkling more brightly now. "Wasn't that a dangerous thing to do?"

"Ah, an eleven-year-old boy knows no fear when it comes to matters of the heart." He leaned back in the chair, enjoying the look of expectancy on Colette's face. "That afternoon Jenny showed up with several of her girlfriends, and we all went out to the pasture where the bull was kept."

"Did you have a red cape?"

"Nope...my father's red long underwear." He was rewarded by her laughter, and his desire for her once again flared to the surface. "Anyway, I got out in the pasture, with Jenny and her friends hanging on the fence, and I waved that underwear at that snorting mass of rage and muscle."

"And what happened?" she asked, leaning forward slightly, all self-consciousness gone.

"That bull charged me and I turned tail and ran, but I couldn't outrun him and somehow he got his horns in the seat of my pants and ripped them right off me. There I was, buck naked in front of the love of my life."

Colette clapped a hand over her mouth, but a giggle escaped her. "You're making that up," she accused.

He held up his hand. "Boy Scout's honor. Not only did I suffer complete and total humiliation in front of the girl I loved, but my dad grounded me for two weeks, told me he couldn't believe he'd raised a son dumber than a post."

They were still laughing a moment later when Gina arrived home. She paused in the doorway of the kitchen. "Looks like the two of you are having fun," she exclaimed.

"Your brother has been telling me about his bull-fighting days," Colette said.

Gina rolled her eyes and joined them at the table. "I've heard that story a hundred times. Jenny is a hairdresser in Foxrun's only beauty shop, and she loves to tell it to her customers."

Tanner leaned back in his chair once again, noticing that now that Gina had arrived home, Colette seemed more relaxed and less on edge. "It would have never worked between Jenny and me," he said. "I could never be happy with a woman who took pleasure in telling others about my humiliation."

"How was your evening?" Colette asked Gina.

Gina smiled, her eyes lighting with obvious pleasure. "It was wonderful. Danny's father is funny, and his mother is so warm and loving. His brothers and sisters are a hoot, and dinner was a wonderful, chaotic madhouse."

As Tanner listened to Gina enthusiastically sharing the events of her evening with Danny's family, he couldn't help but grieve over the fact that he hadn't been able to provide her with the same kind of family background.

"They're a wonderful family," Gina said. "And it's obvious they all love each other very much."

"I'm glad you had a good time," Tanner said, shoving aside the guilt he felt over something he'd had no control over.

"So, what did you two do this evening?" she asked.

Instantly Colette's cheeks brightened with guilty color. "Nothing," she said forcefully. "I mean, we ate at Antonio's, then came here and had coffee."

Gina looked at her for a long moment, then turned and looked at her brother suspiciously. "So, was it good?"

"Was what good?" Colette asked, her voice a full octave higher as the color in her cheeks deepened. She looks guilty as hell, Tanner thought with an indulgent amusement.

"The food at Antonio's," Gina replied, then shook her head. "What did you think I was talking about?"

"I don't know...I think I'm overtired," Colette replied. "And the food was wonderful." She stood and carried her coffee cup and saucer to the sink. "And now I think I'm going to call it a night. Thank you, Tanner, for a lovely dinner."

"Trust me, the pleasure was all mine," he replied, and was rewarded with a new blush stealing over her features. She murmured a good-night and left the kitchen.

Instantly Tanner was granted a mental image of her sliding between her sheets, her naked body gleaming in the moonlight.

He shook his head to dispel the vision and tried to focus on Gina, who was talking about her evening once again, her face glowing with her joy.

For the first time since he'd arrived in Kansas City, he wondered if he was doing the right thing in trying to get Gina to return to the ranch.

Of course you are, a small voice scoffed inside his head. Leaving Gina here didn't necessarily mean she could claim Danny's family as her own. Besides, he didn't want her doing that. She was far too young to tie herself down to any one man. She needed to be back at the ranch to finish her education. She needed to be back at the ranch with him.

As he once again thought of Colette, he realized that for the past couple of days he'd lost his focus. He'd somehow become involved in Colette instead of Gina. He'd been in Kansas City for an entire week and was no closer to getting Gina to come home.

He'd been distracted by Colette's flashing dimple, her sexy curves and her melodic laughter. But it was time for him to get back to the ranch, time to put Colette's charms behind him and focus on his reason for being in Kansas City.

Chapter Eight

Colette couldn't remember the last time she'd been so mortified. But along with her embarrassment was an intense relief that at least one of them had shown some sense.

Tanner had been right. If they had made love she would have regretted it immediately afterward. Still, as she snuggled into her bed, her body still tingled and felt overly warm from his caresses. Her mouth still hungered for his.

He would have been a wonderful lover. She was certain about that. He would have swept her completely out of this world with his passion and tenderness.

However, if that had happened, it would only have made it more difficult to tell him goodbye. And eventually she would have to tell him goodbye. He had a life of his own, and his reasons for being in Kansas City had nothing to do with her.

Besides, she had no intention of becoming weak and dependent on any man. She had no intention of falling in love…ever.

She rolled over on her back and placed her hand on her tummy. Here was another reason not to make love with Tanner. If they had made love, and if she wasn't pregnant now, she could have gotten pregnant by Tanner.

She closed her eyes, trying to imagine what Tanner's and her child would look like. Her mind filled with a vision of a little boy and a little girl with dark hair and big brown eyes.

They would be beautiful children, and Tanner would make a wonderful father. She'd seen his love for Gina and knew his heart would embrace his children. But she wasn't the woman to give him those children, and she knew without doubt that Tanner would heartily disapprove of her choice to be artificially inseminated.

She fell asleep and dreamed of Tanner and awakened the next morning with a hollow ache inside her and the knowledge that Tanner was a definite threat to her emotions. It was time she gained some distance from him.

Over the next several days she didn't have to worry about distancing herself from him. Apparently, he had the same idea. Although she learned from Gina that she had lunch each day with her brother before coming into work, Tanner himself stayed away from the store.

Colette was kept busy. The weather was perfect and business boomed. She had planned a grand opening of sorts that Friday to show off the new kiddie area in the back of the store. Mike had promised her the work would be completed by Thursday evening, and he was as good as his promise.

It was just before seven when she closed down the shop. She'd sent Gina home earlier, wanting some time to arrange the little picnic tables and benches and set out the books and puzzles she'd bought for the children's entertainment.

She'd ordered cookies and pastries from Johnny's Café to be picked up in the morning, and a 20-percent-off-anything-in-the-store coupon had run in the local papers that day, good for the opening the next day.

There was only one thing she wanted to do before she began arranging everything for the following day. Sitting down at the register counter, she picked up the phone and punched in her mother's phone number.

She had left two messages in the past two days on Lillian's machine, telling her about the grand opening and how she would love to have her mother attend. So far, she hadn't heard from Lillian.

She sat up straighter as she heard her mother answer. "Lillian," she said in greeting.

"Oh, it's you. I was expecting a call from Joe. We had a little tiff and he drove off a few minutes ago."

"Are you all right?" Colette asked worriedly, knowing how her mother tended to fall apart when there was stress with the man in her life.

"I'm fine. It was just a silly little fight, and I'm sure he'll be calling or coming back any moment. Now, why are you calling?"

"Did you get my messages about my celebration at the store tomorrow?"

"Oh, yes, but honestly, Colette, why would I want to come to a celebration in a baby store?"

Because it's my store, Colette's heart cried out. Because I'm your daughter and you're proud of me. Bitter tears sprang to her eyes despite her determination not to cry. "I just thought you might like to stop by, maybe have a quick cup of coffee and a cookie with me."

"You know that sort of thing isn't my style," Lillian replied, then added, "but I hope you have a nice day. Oh, my other line is ringing, maybe that's Joe."

"Then I'll just say goodbye now," Colette said before realizing her mother had already clicked over to answer the other call.

Slowly Colette hung up the receiver and cursed herself when tears began seeping from her eyes. Why did she continue to be disappointed by Lillian? Why did she continue to want more, need more than Lillian could give...had ever been able to give?

The tears turned to sobs, and she vowed this was the last time Lillian would ever make her cry. But this latest disappointment felt like the demise of a fantasy she'd entertained for far too long...and fantasies were always difficult to let go of.

She'd never felt so alone. She'd wanted to share her success, but she realized now she had nobody to share it with. She'd wanted her mother to see the store in full swing, filled with customers and children, but she should have known that Lillian had never much cared about what Colette was doing with her life.

A knock on the shop door shot her up to a standing position. Tanner stood outside. He waved, indicating he saw her and she hastily swiped at her tears. He was probably here to walk Gina home, not knowing that Colette had sent the young woman home early.

The smile on Tanner's face faded as she unlocked the door and opened it. "Gina isn't here," Colette said. "I sent her home early today."

"What's wrong?" he asked, and stepped into the shop.

"Nothing," she denied quickly. "Nothing is wrong."

He placed his hands on her shoulders, his beautiful blue eyes filled with tenderness. "You've been crying."

"No...I just...you know...allergies in the Midwest.'' She tried to twist away from him, but he held her shoulders tight.

''Colette.'' His voice was so gentle it acted as a catalyst and more tears sprang to her eyes. ''Talk to me, sweetie. What's made you so sad?''

''Please…it's nothing,'' she said, and succeeded in breaking away from him.

'' 'Nothing' doesn't make tears,'' he replied softly. ''Talk to me, honey. Tell me what's going on.'' He reached for her once again, and this time she went into his embrace and hid her face in his chest.

His chambray shirt smelled of a combination of fabric softener and male and the cologne scent she'd come to identify as belonging solely to Tanner.

She drew a deep breath and fought to control the tears that seemed to have an endless supply, but she was unsuccessful.

As Tanner's arms wrapped around her and held her tight, sobs broke free once again. He patted her back, murmuring soothing words as she cried for the mother she'd never had.

It was several minutes before she finally managed to get herself under better control and stepped out of his embrace with a small embarrassed laugh.

''I'm sorry,'' she exclaimed. ''I don't know what's wrong with me. Normally I don't react this way.'' In the back of her mind she wondered if this was the first symptom of being pregnant. She'd heard the stories of pregnancy turning women into hormonal messes.

"React to what?" he asked gently.

"My mother," she confessed. She took another step back from him, still embarrassed that he'd seen her in an uncharacteristically weak moment. "I don't know why I continually set myself up to be disappointed by her. You would think eventually I'd be smart and learn to accept her as she is."

"And exactly how is she?" he asked.

Colette sank down on the stool behind the register. "Cold...uncaring, without any maternal instincts. She's a woman who should never have had a child. And my mistake is that I keep trying to make her into something she isn't, then I get disappointed."

Tanner moved to stand on the opposite side of the counter from where she was seated. He leaned forward, propping his elbows on the countertop as he gazed at her. "So what happened tonight?"

Colette shrugged. "It's so silly, really. I called and invited her to the big celebration tomorrow, but she doesn't want to come." She looked at him. "I knew she wouldn't. I don't even know why I invited her."

"Because there's still a little girl inside you hungry for your mother," he said, his voice achingly gentle. "I know that hunger. My mother has been gone a long time and there are still moments when I miss her so much."

She reached across the counter and touched his hand lightly. "I'm sorry your mother is gone."

He smiled. "And I'm sorry your mother can't be what you need."

"Would you like to see the new area?" Colette asked, deciding a change in topic was necessary. "Mike finished the work earlier today and I was just about to make sure everything was in order."

"Sure," he agreed.

Together they walked toward the back of the shop. Colette had told herself all week that she was glad he had stayed away from the shop, that it was better if they distanced themselves from each other. Now she realized how much she'd missed him.

She'd missed his sexy smile and the warmth of his impossibly blue eyes. She'd missed his conversation and the sound of his laughter.

As they reached the new play area, her heart expanded with pride. Mike had done a tremendous job. A small slide stood in one corner of the fenced section, and on the other side were two little picnic tables and benches.

"It looks like a miniature park," Tanner said. "All that you are lacking is a couple of trees or bushes around the edges."

She nodded. "I was going to try to pick up some potted plants this week, but I just haven't had time."

"This was a terrific idea," Tanner replied, his

words shooting a warmth of pride through her. "The parents who shop here are going to love it."

"Thanks," she replied and picked up the stack of books to distribute at the tables. He followed her example and picked up the pile of puzzles. "You don't have to do that," she protested.

He grinned. "It's not exactly a difficult job." He began to place the puzzles on the tables.

"Speaking of difficult jobs, how is your crusade to take Gina back to Foxrun coming along?"

His smile was instantly replaced with a frown. "I always knew Gina was stubborn, but I had no idea she could be this stubborn."

Finished with the puzzles, he leaned against the slide and continued. "Monday at lunch I tried guilt. I told her how important her finishing her degree was to me and how Mom and Dad would have wanted her to complete her education."

Colette finished with the books and perched on one of the small benches. "Didn't work?"

"Not by a long shot," he replied. "Then Tuesday I ordered her back home. But she left in the middle of the meal, told me I was being mean."

"And Wednesday at lunch?"

"Bribery." He grinned wickedly. "Gina has always wanted a vintage Thunderbird convertible. I told her if she'd come back to the ranch and finish college, I'd buy her one."

"Wow, that's quite a bribe," she replied.

"Yeah, but it didn't work. She said she'd rather have her independence than a car."

"And today?"

He gave her a sheepish grin. "She refused to have lunch with me." Colette laughed. "Are you done for the night?" he asked. She nodded. "Come on, I'll walk you home."

It took only minutes for her to lock up the shop and together they started back to her apartment building. As they walked, they talked, sharing thoughts about mothers and fathers and the important roles they played in children's lives.

He also talked about the ranch, and she heard the homesickness in his voice and knew it was probably only a matter of days before he would be gone.

It frightened her...the hollow ache that filled her heart as she thought of never seeing Tanner again. And it was at that moment she realized with horror that she was falling in love with him.

Tanner rode shotgun in the greenhouse truck, whistling beneath his breath as they headed toward Colette's shop. It was just after seven-thirty and the sun was already bright overhead, promising a beautiful day for Colette's celebration sale.

Colette. He'd tried desperately to distance himself from her after the night they'd nearly made love. Instead of spending time at her shop, he'd wandered the city, seeing the tourist attractions. But she'd never been far from his thoughts.

His thoughts hadn't been just of how soft her skin had been, how sweet her mouth had tasted, but also of the intelligence that shone from her eyes, the quick wit that made him laugh.

She was an amazingly strong woman and yet intensely vulnerable and sensitive. Seeing her tears the night before, holding her in his arms as she'd wept about her mother, had touched him deeply. He'd wanted to find Lillian Carson and shake her until she realized what a gift she had in her daughter.

He'd awakened that morning knowing what he wanted to do for Colette and had immediately sought out a greenhouse. He'd taken a taxi to the tree nursery that one of the hotel clerks had recommended, pleased to find it open and available to make an immediate delivery.

In the bed of the truck were two potted miniature rosebushes and two small dogwood trees with glorious white blossoms.

He smiled as he imagined Colette's reaction. Surely she would be thrilled. The trees and bushes would be perfect to complete the parklike aura of her kiddy area.

"Up there on the right," he said to the driver, a young kid who looked barely old enough to have his driver's license.

The kid, who wore a name tag that read Bobby,

pulled up at the curb in front of the Little Bit Baby Boutique. "What time does it open?" he asked, obviously noticing the darkness of the store and the Closed sign on the door.

"Not for an hour or so," Tanner replied. "But I don't expect you to wait. If we can just unload them on the sidewalk out front, then I'll move them inside when the store opens."

Bobby nodded and together the two men got out of the truck. It took only minutes to unload the bed of the truck, then Bobby took off to head back to the greenhouse.

Tanner knew Colette would get to the store early today. She would be eager to set up the cookies and pastries for her customers.

He hoped the day would be successful for her, that the store would be packed with customers from the moment it opened until it closed that evening.

He'd only been standing there about ten minutes when he saw her coming down the sidewalk, her arms laden with bakery boxes. He hurried toward her, his heart opening as he saw the shine of the sun on her curly hair, the length of her shapely legs beneath the spring-green dress she wore.

"What are you doing here so early?" she asked as he took the boxes from her arms.

"It's a big day. I didn't want to miss a minute of it," he replied with a smile.

The beautiful smile she returned to him warmed

him from his head to his toes. But it was on her lips for only a moment, then fell away as they reached the store.

"What's all this?" she asked, looking at the trees and rosebushes.

"It's your park," Tanner replied.

She stared at the items for a long moment, then looked up at him, her brown eyes luminous. "You shouldn't have done that," she exclaimed, and unlocked the door to the shop.

He was surprised by the anger that laced her voice. "If you don't like the kind I selected, I can exchange them for something else," Tanner exclaimed as he hurried after her.

"That's not the point," she replied. She took the pastry boxes from him and set them on the counter. "You don't have to do things for me. I'm perfectly capable of taking care of myself."

This was not exactly the reaction he'd been expecting, and irritation welled up inside him. "I realize you're capable of taking care of yourself. I just wanted to do something nice for you, and a gracious thank-you would have sufficed."

Her cheeks grew pink and she looked away from him. "I apologize," she said softly. "And I should be ashamed of myself."

"Yes, you should," he agreed, his irritation with her dissipating instantly. "And now I've got two rosebushes and two dogwood trees that need a home.

Should I bring them inside or call the nursery and tell them to pick them back up?''

She smiled impishly, causing her dimple to dance provocatively. ''Why don't you bring the trees and bushes inside and call the nursery to pick me up.''

He laughed. ''Not on your life. I'm not about to take over the job of selling diapers and booties to pregnant women.''

As he went back outside to carry in the greenery, Colette set up a card table just inside the door and started a large coffeepot and set out the pastries.

By the time Tanner had all the potted plants inside, she had finished with her arrangement of the goodies for the day. She walked back to the kiddy area and directed him where to place the plants, then together they walked back to the front of the store and poured themselves a cup of coffee.

Colette looked at her wristwatch and paced around the store, straightening displays and refolding blankets. Tanner recognized her restlessness as nerves and knew today was far more important to her than he'd initially realized.

''Come sit down, Colette,'' he instructed. He grabbed her hand and pointed her to the chair behind the counter. ''It's going to be a great day for you, and all the pacing and nervous energy expended isn't going to do anything but make you tired before you even open the doors.''

She sat and smiled at him. ''I don't know why I'm

so nervous. Today is probably going to be just like any other day of business.''

"Only better," he replied.

"From your lips to God's ears."

At that moment Gina appeared. She pushed open the door of the shop, greeted both Tanner and Colette, then grabbed one of the bootie-shaped cookies from the table. "Hmm, these are great," she exclaimed after taking a bite.

"Glad you like them, because if we don't have any customers today that's what we'll be eating for supper for the next couple of weeks," Colette replied.

However, Colette's worries were for nothing. Within minutes of opening the doors for the day, the place began to fill with people.

Not only were Colette and Gina kept busy, but Tanner found himself working, as well, greeting people, checking occasionally on the children who were enjoying the kiddy area and waiting on customers while the two women helped others.

The morning flew by and it wasn't until after two that afternoon that they enjoyed their first lull. "Why don't I run down to Johnny's Café and grab some hamburgers?" Tanner suggested.

"Sounds good to me," Gina said.

"I'm not really very hungry," Colette replied. She sat down on the chair and heaved a sigh of exhaustion.

Tanner eyed her critically. "You have to eat," he said. "Did you eat supper last night?"

She frowned thoughtfully. "No," she admitted.

"And what about breakfast this morning?"

Her frown deepened. "No, I had so many things on my mind."

"Then I'm getting you a hamburger, and if you won't eat it, I'll personally force-feed you," he warned.

"And he will, too," Gina assured Colette. "He's a regular mother hen when it comes to eating three squares a day and getting a good night's sleep."

"That's right, and after I feed you there's nothing I'd like better than to tuck you in."

Tanner heard Colette's gasp and Gina's hoot of laughter as he left the shop and headed for Johnny's. Over and over again Colette had said and given indications that she was capable of taking care of herself, that she wanted nothing more than her independence.

But Tanner had never met a woman who needed to be taken care of more than Colette. She not only needed somebody to take care of her physically, but she needed somebody to support her emotionally, somebody to share in her successes and failures.

As he'd held her the night before and she'd cried about her mother, he'd wanted to be that caring, supportive person for her. He'd wanted to hold her tight enough that hurt could never find her heart again.

It worried him just a little, the protectiveness she evoked in him. That, coupled with the desire he felt for her, was a heady combination of emotions that made him distinctly uncomfortable.

As he'd worked in the boutique, helping expectant mothers and fathers, he'd found himself wondering what it would be like to be expecting a child. He'd looked at the booties and little T-shirts, the soft pastel-colored blankets and frilly dresses, and a deep yearning had sprung up inside him.

Suddenly he was struck with an overwhelming homesickness for Two Hearts. Things were much less complicated at the ranch, and it was past time that he resume his life there.

As he entered Johnny's Café, he reached a decision. If he couldn't convince Gina to return home with him, then on Sunday he would go back by himself.

That gave him two days to get through to Gina... and two days to get Colette out of his head and his heart.

Chapter Nine

"Go home," Gina urged Colette at just after six o'clock that evening. "I can stay the last hour and close up by myself."

Colette hesitated. The idea of leaving and going home and putting her feet up sounded positively wonderful. The day had far exceeded her expectations. It had been the busiest day she'd had since first opening the store.

"Go," Gina commanded. "You look exhausted and I can handle things until close."

"Are you sure?" Colette asked. The crowd had dissipated, and no customers were in the store at the current time.

"Positive," Gina assured her.

"All right," Colette said, capitulating. "I have to admit, I'm more than a little bit exhausted."

"You probably stayed awake all night worrying about today," Gina said.

"I was awake most of the night. I'll fix something for dinner and have it waiting for you when you get home."

Gina nodded. "Sounds good, I'm starting to get hungry." Colette grabbed her purse, gave Gina last-minute instructions on what to do with the leftover pastries, then left the shop.

She had been awake most of the night before, only it hadn't been just worry about today that had kept her awake. Thoughts of Tanner had continually played in her mind.

She'd sensed his restlessness and knew it was only a matter of time before he returned to Two Hearts. And it bothered her how much she was going to miss him.

That moment the day before when she'd realized she'd fallen in love with him had utterly stunned her, and she'd hugged the warmth of that love to her breast all night long.

However, it was a love she intended to do nothing about. Her life was planned and there was no room for a man in it—not even a man who made her knees weaken and her pulse pound. She would have her baby and her business...and that's all she needed to be happy.

She leaned tiredly against the wall of the elevator

as it carried her up to her eighth-floor apartment, trying to dismiss thoughts of Tanner from her mind.

However, trying to stop thinking about Tanner was like trying to stop breathing. He filled her head, filled her heart...filled her very soul.

She'd allowed him to get closer than she'd ever allowed anyone else in her life, and now she regretted it, for she knew when he left she would mourn what might have been.

It was impossible for her to know exactly what Tanner felt for her. She knew he desired her, but she wasn't sure his feelings went any deeper than a healthy lust.

But even if they did, even if he fell down on one knee and offered to whisk her off her feet and carry her to his ranch to live forever and always, she wouldn't go.

She'd seen the negative side of love up close and personal, and it was not pretty. She would never give herself an opportunity to become like her mother—needy, clinging and weak. She would never become a woman who built her entire life, her entire world, around a man.

The minute she opened her apartment door she kicked off her shoes and flopped down on the sofa, exhaustion sweeping through her.

She thought of the pregnancy test in her bathroom cabinet. It had been almost four weeks since she'd

had the procedure to make her pregnant. It was possible it would show up on a test now.

But at the moment she didn't have the energy to
take the test. Besides, it would probably be more ac-
curate if she waited another couple of days.

Her monthly cycle had been due a week ago, but
she knew better than to depend on that as an indica-
tion of pregnancy. Her periods had always been ir-
regular.

She closed her eyes, deciding she would rest just a
few minutes before getting up and checking out what
she was going to cook for supper.

She awakened suddenly, surprised by how easily
she'd fallen asleep. The apartment had darkened and
she realized she must have been asleep for some time.

Sitting up, she checked her wristwatch, shocked to
see that it was just after eight. Gina should be home
at any moment. The shop closed at seven-thirty, and
normally the young woman would have already been
home, but tonight she would have to wrap up the
leftover pastries and wash out the industrial-size coffeemaker.

Colette went into the kitchen and opened the refrigerator door and stared at the contents. She didn't
feel like cooking supper. She shut the fridge door and
walked back into the living room and ordered a pizza.

With a delivery time of half an hour, she hurried
into her bathroom and jumped into the shower, then
dressed in her nightshirt and a robe.

Checking her watch again, she wondered where Gina was? It shouldn't have taken her that long to close up. She picked up the phone and dialed the number to the store.

She let it ring five times, then hung up. Apparently Gina had already left and would probably be walking through the door at any minute.

As she waited for Gina and the pizza, she tried to keep thoughts of Tanner at bay, but her mind refused to cooperate with her desire not to think of him.

What would it be like to live at Two Hearts and be loved for the rest of her life by Tanner? What would it be like to have his children, share his life? Each time he'd talked about Foxrun to her, the picture he'd painted of his life there had filled her with a wistful yearning.

Why…why did these thoughts torment her so?

He'd been a tremendous help at the shop all day, pitching in when the crowd got big, supervising the play area and giving a male opinion for the women shoppers who wanted one.

It had been around three when he'd left, telling her and Gina that he needed to make some phone calls and take care of some business at the ranch.

Thoughts of Tanner disappeared as the doorbell rang. She opened the door to a familiar, smiling young man holding a large pizza box. "Evening, Ms. Carson," he said.

"Hi, Ralph." Ralph had often delivered pizza to

Colette. His father owned the pizza place where Colette placed her orders.

"I guess it's a no-cooking night," he said as they exchanged pizza for cash.

"You've got that right. I decided to treat myself to one of your father's creative masterpieces."

Ralph laughed. "Well, this masterpiece is just the way you like it...with lots of extra pepperoni."

"Thanks, Ralph, and tell your dad I said hi." He nodded and with a wave headed back to the elevator as Colette closed and relocked her apartment door.

The scent of rich, tangy sauce and spicy pepperoni filled the air as Colette placed the pizza in the center of the table. Now all she had to do was wait for Gina to get home.

The minutes ticked by. Colette set the table, made a pitcher of iced tea and still no Gina. Maybe Danny stopped by the store and they decided to grab a bite to eat, she told herself.

Gina was an independent adult. It was ridiculous for Colette to worry because she wasn't home yet. But as the minutes continued to tick by, she couldn't help the worry that fluttered through her.

By nine her concern was impossible to ignore. Gina was a conscientious young lady and always called when she made plans and was going to be home late.

As two single women living alone, Colette had always stressed how important it was that they each have an idea of what the other was doing or who they might be with. Besides, she'd mentioned to Gina that she'd have something ready to eat when she got home, and the young woman hadn't mentioned any other plans.

So, where was she? Why hadn't she called? By the time ten o'clock rolled around, Colette knew she had to do something.

She sat down next to the phone and clicked her fingernails on the plastic receiver. If nothing was wrong, then Gina would probably be angry that Colette had called in the cavalry. But there was no way Colette could ignore her unease and just sit around and wait for Gina to return.

Drawing a deep breath, she picked up the phone, punched in the numbers for information and asked for the number to Tanner's hotel.

Tanner had just showered and crawled into bed when the phone rang. It took him a moment to answer as he fumbled on the nightstand for the phone. "Hello?"

"Tanner?"

He rolled over and turned on the bedside lamp. "Colette."

"I'm sorry to bother you," she said.

It was obvious from her tone of voice that she was not pleased to be calling him. "You aren't bothering me," he assured her, then waited expectantly.

"Tanner, it's probably nothing, but I'm a little bit worried about Gina."

Instantly adrenaline flooded through him and he sat up. "What do you mean? Worried about what?"

There was a long pause. "She isn't home yet."

"Home yet? You mean home from the shop?" He looked at the alarm clock on the nightstand. "Was she keeping the shop open late tonight?"

"No, and I've called there several times and there's no answer."

"Did she have a date with Danny after work?"

"She didn't mention anything about a date. Right before I left the shop, I told her I'd have something to eat ready for her when she got home, and she didn't mention anything about not coming directly home."

Fear, rich and sickening, slammed through him. "I'll be right over," he said, and without giving her an opportunity to say anything more he hung up.

He grabbed his jeans and ripped them on, then did the same with his shirt. As he pulled on socks and his boots, frantic worry rocked through him.

If Gina had closed up the shop at the normal time, that meant she'd been missing for over two and a half hours. Where could she be?

Before going to Colette's apartment building, he raced the three blocks from his hotel to the shop. As he ran, his heart pounded frantically, his mind filling with horrifying possibilities.

When he reached the shop he found the interior

dark and the front door locked. Nothing looked amiss, and a quick look around the entire perimeter of the building yielded no clues.

He hurried on to Colette's apartment, cursing the vivid imagination that presented all kinds of terrible visions in his head.

Had somebody snatched her off the street as she'd walked home? Was she right now in the hands of a madman? Or had she simply gone off somewhere and neglected to tell Colette? In either case she was in a world of trouble.

He didn't have to bother knocking on Colette's door. The moment he stepped off the elevator, she opened the door to admit him into the apartment.

"Any word from her?" he asked.

She shook her head, looking unusually small and fragile in a pale pink robe, her face etched with light lines of tension. "Maybe we should call the police?" she suggested, toying nervously with the belt of her robe.

Tanner raked a hand through his hair and expelled a sigh. "They'd laugh us into next week. At this point all we could tell them is that she's twenty-one years old and is a few hours late for supper. They won't do anything until she's been missing at least twenty-four hours."

Colette sank down on the edge of the sofa, her forehead still wrinkled with furrows of worry. "So what should we do?"

Tanner moved to the bank of windows and paced back and forth. "Do you remember Danny's last name?"

"Burlington."

He stifled a groan. There were probably a million Burlingtons listed in the Kansas City phone directory.

"We know he lives nearby, so I could probably figure out which Burlington it is," she said as if she'd read his thoughts.

"You have a phone book?" he asked, for the first time feeling a wave of hope.

She nodded and went into the kitchen. Tanner followed right behind her. Surely Gina was with Danny. With the thoughtlessness of youth she hadn't realized anyone would worry.

Colette pulled a phone book from a cabinet and opened it on the kitchen table, seeking the pages that would have the numbers for all the Burlingtons in the city.

Tanner moved to stand next to her, vaguely aware of the sweet, clean scent of her and the warmth of her curves against him as he pressed closer to view the numbers.

She ran a well-manicured pink fingernail down the page, scanning the numbers in what appeared to be surprising speed.

"Here's a possibility," she said. Tanner moved from her side to the phone and punched in the number as she read it off to him.

It was the wrong Burlington.

They called four numbers. Three of them didn't know a Danny and nobody answered at the fourth place. Tanner was just hanging up the receiver when they heard the front door open and close.

Gina walked into the kitchen and there was a moment of stunned silence. Her bottom lip was slightly swollen, her hair was in disarray, her panty hose were in shreds and her knees were bloodied.

"Don't panic," she exclaimed hurriedly. "It looks much worse than it is."

Despite her words, it was sheer panic that shot through Tanner. In three quick strides he was before her, and he grabbed her by the shoulders to assure himself that she was really all right.

For a moment he couldn't speak. No question seemed as important as hugging her to his chest, assuring himself that she was really okay. It was only after a long, fierce bear hug that he stepped back. "What happened?"

She broke free from him and set her purse on the table. "A little weasel tried to snatch my purse."

"How did your knees get so skinned up?" Colette asked.

"When he grabbed for it, he didn't realize it was looped over my head and I fell." She smiled faintly. "I think I scared him more than he scared me. I was screaming like a banshee and I managed to hit him with a couple of shots of my pepper spray. I went right down to the police station to make a report. That's where I've been all this time. I tried to call but the line was busy, then decided I'd just explain when I got home.''

Fear grappled with rage inside Tanner as he stared at his baby sister. ''Pack your bags,'' he said curtly. ''You are not staying in a place where you get mugged and have to carry pepper spray.''

Gina sank down in a chair at the table. ''Don't be ridiculous,'' she scoffed. ''I'll do no such thing.''

Tanner's anger increased. The frustration he'd felt for the past two weeks where she was concerned exploded. He'd tried to be patient, had tried to make her see things his way without being harsh, but now his patience was shot.

''Gina, for God's sake, you could have been killed,'' he exclaimed, residual fear still strong and bold inside him.

''But I wasn't,'' Gina replied. ''I handled it just fine.''

''This time…but what about next time?'' Tanner wanted to bellow, he wanted to grab her by the shoulders and shake some sense into her. ''I mean it, Gina. I'm leaving here Sunday morning and you will be beside me in that truck.''

Gina rose. ''I don't want to fight with you now, Tanner. What I need is a nice, relaxing bath, so I'll just tell you good-night now.''

Without another word she left the kitchen. Tanner

turned his frustrated gaze to Colette. "I don't know how to make her understand. She's so damned stubborn."

The corners of Colette's lips turned upward. "Gee, I wonder where she gets that?" The smile fell away, and her warm brown eyes were filled with sympathy. "Maybe she'll think differently in the morning."

"I hope so." He sighed. Now that the tenseness of the moment had passed, he was exhausted. "I better get out of here so you can get some sleep."

Together they walked from the kitchen to the front door. "So, you're really leaving Sunday morning?"

"Yeah, it's past time I get back home." He gazed at her, for a moment wishing he wasn't taking one young woman back to Foxrun with him, but two.

At the moment Colette looked as beautiful as he'd ever seen her. Her brown eyes were luminous and the pink robe accentuated her creamy complexion.

He wanted to wrap her up in his arms and carry her to his truck, take her back to his ranch and fill the well of need he sensed inside her. But of course he couldn't do that. She had a life here and a business to run.

"I'll miss you, Tanner." She said the words slowly, as if with great reluctance.

He took a step closer to her. "And I'll miss you."

Without conscious thought, he reached for her.

One last kiss, he told himself as he claimed her

mouth. One last moment of savoring the sweet delight of kissing Colette.

The frustration of moments before fell aside as desire ached inside him. He didn't just want to take her home with him, he wanted to take her home and keep her in his bed for at least a month. He wanted to wake up each morning with her in his arms and fall asleep at night after making love to her.

He broke the kiss, knowing his thoughts were foolish and to continue kissing her would only make leaving more difficult.

"Good night, Colette," he said as he released her, then before he could say or do anything more foolish, he left.

"There's nothing better than cold pizza," Gina exclaimed as she grabbed another piece from the box in the middle of the kitchen table.

It was just after midnight as the two ate the pizza that had been ordered hours before. Gina had taken a bath and put antiseptic on her skinned knees, and other than a touch of body soreness from her unexpected fall, she seemed none the worse for wear.

On the other hand, Colette had done nothing but think since Tanner had left. Her initial thoughts had been of intense sadness. He was leaving day after tomorrow, and she'd never again hear his laughter, never again see passion in the depths of those beautiful blue eyes.

As Gina had bathed, Colette's thoughts had turned to her. The trauma that Gina had suffered had horrified her, and for the first time ever Colette wondered if Gina wasn't making a huge mistake in not returning home with her brother who loved her so.

Watching Tanner wrap Gina in his arms and hug her with such obvious love and concern had touched Colette deeply. She couldn't help but think of all the times in her past she'd wished somebody had wrapped her up and hugged her with that same kind of love.

"Gina, maybe you should reconsider your decision to go back with Tanner," she now said.

Gina set down her piece of pizza and stared at Colette with narrowed eyes. "What are you talking about?"

Colette shrugged. "You know Tanner only wants the best for you. Maybe it would be a good idea for you to spend another year at the ranch, finish up your teaching degree and not have to worry about paying rent or getting mugged."

"He got to you." Gina laughed without humor. "I should have known he would. He's been subtly seducing you the whole time he's been here just to get you on his side."

"That's ridiculous," Colette scoffed, although she couldn't control the sickening disappointment that rolled through her as Gina's words imploded inside her.

"What's ridiculous about it?" Gina shoved away from the table, a look of disgust on her face. "Tanner doesn't like to lose and he'd do anything to increase his odds of winning, and the best way for him to win is to get you on his side." She stood. "Face it, Colette, you've been played." With these words she stalked out of the kitchen, and a moment later Colette heard the slam of her bedroom door.

Chapter Ten

Early Sunday morning Colette paced back and forth in her living room. She expected Tanner to arrive at any moment. He thought he was going to pick up Gina, but what he was going to get instead was a large piece of Colette's anger.

Since Friday night, when Gina had told her she'd been played by Tanner, her anger had grown by the minute. At first she hadn't believed what Gina had said, but the more she dwelled on it, the more she began to believe Gina's words.

If he'd truly felt something for her and hadn't just been trying to manipulate her, then why hadn't he made love to her when she had been so out of control from his kisses, his caresses. If he'd felt the same, he wouldn't have been able to stop himself from making love to her.

But instead he had called things to a halt. He hadn't been willing to take his manipulation of her to that length. She'd been grateful that he hadn't shown his face in the store the day before.

The hurt of Gina's words had been too close to the surface. His kisses had felt so real, her heart had cried out. His desire for her had seemed so genuine.

Now she'd managed to shove the hurt aside and instead simply felt a slow burn of anger.

She poured herself another cup of coffee. It was just after seven, and she had no idea when to expect Tanner, but she had a feeling it would be soon, for he'd want to get an early start back to Foxrun.

Gina had left at the crack of dawn, choosing avoidance over confrontation with her brother. Danny had come by for her, and the two had planned to go out for an early breakfast, then spend the day at the park.

Colette was grateful the young girl wasn't here. Despite her desire to the contrary, she already felt tears building inside her as she thought of never seeing Tanner Rothman again.

It was ridiculous, really. She'd never wanted a man in her life, had refused to ever consider the possibility of marriage. But there had been moments when Tanner had talked about the ranch and the small-town living that had sent a deep yearning through her.

She took a sip of her coffee, then touched her tummy. Okay, so she wouldn't have a husband to hold her through the night, and she wouldn't live in a charming little town where everyone knew everyone. But she would have her family. Her baby would be her family and that's all she would ever need. Her baby would get all the love and all the attention and would never have to come second place to any man.

She jumped and sloshed coffee over the rim of her mug as the doorbell rang. Setting the mug on the kitchen table, she steeled herself for her final goodbye to Tanner.

As usual, he was clad in a pair of tight jeans and a navy T-shirt that deepened the impossible blue of his eyes. The sight of him created a deep ache in her heart, an ache she'd never experienced before.

"She's not here," she said without preamble. "She told me to tell you she loves you, but she's tired of fighting with you and she's not returning to Foxrun."

He stepped into the living room and muttered a curse beneath his breath. "I told her to be packed and ready to go."

"And you thought it would be as easy as that? My, you are arrogant."

He looked at her and frowned. "What bee crawled into your bonnet?"

"No bee," she replied, and moved several steps back from him so she couldn't smell his dear, familiar scent. "I just can't believe that you issued a command and really expected Gina to comply just like that."

"She knows I want her to come back to the ranch."

"And when are you going to really listen to what

she wants?'' Colette's anger with him sprang to the surface, although she wasn't particularly angry with how he'd handled things with Gina, this was a perfect opportunity to vent some of that anger. ''You've raised her to be strong and independent and to believe in herself. Why can't you let her do that?''

''I will let her do that—when it's time.'' He shoved his hands in his pockets, frustration etched across his forehead.

''It's time now, Tanner. You need to let her go.''

His frown of frustration deepened into a scowl. ''You don't know what you're talking about.''

''Yes, I do,'' she retorted, and took another step back from him. ''I know you've tried threats and bribes to get her to go back with you.'' She narrowed her gaze. ''And I know you played me like a fiddle to get me on your side so the two of us could force her into complying with your wishes.''

He pulled his hands out of his pockets and looked at her in confusion. ''What do you mean I played you like a fiddle?''

Colette felt the burn of her cheeks. ''All your flirting with me, all the sweet talk, all the kisses, it was all about manipulation.''

He stared at her for a long moment, and she thought she saw a faint touch of color appear in his cheeks. Guilt, she thought with a renewed burst of pain.

In three long strides he was mere inches from her.

He took her by the shoulders and held tight when she twisted to get away from him. "Colette." He said her name softly, then drew a deep breath. "I'll admit that the first night we all went out to dinner, the idea of using you to get to Gina did cross my mind."

Pain seared through Colette as he confirmed what Gina had told her. She twisted again, needing to get away from his touch, his nearness as tears suddenly burned at her eyes.

"But, honey, I promise you every kiss I gave you was about my desire, not Gina. Every caress I gave you was about my need, not Gina." His expression was soft and gentle and she was more than a little frightened at how desperately she wanted to believe him.

"It doesn't make any difference," she replied, and this time when she turned her shoulders to escape his grasp, he released her.

She wanted to be angry with him, needed her anger to wrap her in a cocoon of ire where her hurt couldn't reach her. And she wanted to make him mad. It would be so much easier if they parted acrimoniously—then perhaps telling him goodbye wouldn't hurt so much.

"In fact, last night I officially made Gina my assistant manager and gave her a nice raise to go with the title," she said.

His eyes darkened to the ominous shade of thunderclouds. "Why in the hell did you do that?"

Colette walked to the sofa and perched on the edge, ready to spring back up if necessary. "Because she deserved it. In the time she has been working for me, she's proven herself to be responsible and trustworthy. She's bright and hardworking and you need to let her go."

Tanner raked a hand through his hair, his frustration obvious in the tension that rolled off him. "You could have worked with me on this."

"Sorry, your kisses weren't good enough to make me put my personal beliefs aside." She folded and unfolded her hands in her lap, wanting to end this discussion for good.

She needed him to get out of her apartment, away from her before her tears began to fall. "You know what I think?" She didn't wait for his response. "I think you want Gina home with you because you're afraid."

"Afraid? That's ridiculous," he scoffed.

"I don't think it's ridiculous. If you don't have Gina at the ranch then all you have left is your own life, and according to Gina, you don't have much of one."

"You don't know what you're talking about," he exclaimed, and took a step toward where she was seated.

She tensed, but continued. "Oh, I think I do. You've built your entire world around her and you're afraid to let her go because you have nothing and nobody else in your life.''

''What do you know about it?'' The storm clouds were back in his eyes and his voice was deep, with a sharp edge. ''What do you know about loving somebody, caring about somebody? You've closed yourself up so tight you refuse to let anyone in your life. You're as dysfunctional as your mother, incapable of loving anyone.''

''That's not true.'' She sprang up from the sofa.

''You told me yourself that you'd never had a serious relationship. You're twenty-eight years old and you hide in your work. You sell baby things to women with families so you can live vicariously through them, but you never put your own heart on the line.''

''That's not true,'' she exclaimed vehemently. ''Just because I don't need a man doesn't mean I won't have my own family and it doesn't mean I'm incapable of loving.''

He smiled thinly. ''If you intend to have a family, then I would bet that sooner or later you are going to need a man.''

''Not in this day and age,'' she fired back. ''In fact, it's very possible that I'm pregnant right now.''

He looked stunned. ''I don't understand,'' he finally said. ''How is that possible?''

''A month ago I was artificially inseminated.''

Her words were met with thick, heavy silence. She

looked away from the censure in his eyes. The anger that she'd so desperately tried to maintain dissipated, leaving behind only a heart filled with pain.

"How could you do that?" he asked with a touch of incredulity. "How could you consciously make the decision to condemn a child to a life without a father?"

He stalked over to her and once again took her by the shoulders, forcing her to look into the eyes that radiated not only deep disapproval but pain, as well.

"Colette, you know what it was like to grow up without a father, and I will miss my father every day for the rest of my life. How could you consciously make a decision to give a child that same sort of emptiness?"

"I can be enough," she said, and raised her chin defiantly. "This baby is going to have all the love I never had."

"That baby will never be able to fill up the holes your mother left in your heart." He released her and stepped back. "I feel sorry for that baby and I feel sorry for you."

"Get out," she demanded, angry tears scalding her cheeks as they fell. "I don't need anything from you, Tanner Rothman, especially not your pity."

"Don't worry, I'm going," he said as he headed toward the door. "But I have one more thing to say to you. You know, Colette, you're never going to be able to fill up the emptiness inside you if you don't admit that you need someone.''

"And I have one more thing to say to you," she replied, some of the anger gone from her voice. "You raised Gina in your own image. You raised her to be strong and capable and self-assured. Trust in what you did with her and let her go.''

For a long moment he gazed at her, and in his eyes she saw something warm and wonderful. She fought the impulse to throw herself into his arms, to tell him that she'd already discovered the need inside herself and she needed him.

"Goodbye, Tanner," she said, and kept her gaze on him steady and strong, not wanting him to see the devastating emotions that filled her.

He turned and grabbed the doorknob and without looking back at her murmured a goodbye, then left the apartment.

Colette felt as if her heart was shattering. She felt it breaking into a million little pieces, and the pain forced a cry from the depths of her.

She sank back down on the sofa, half-blinded by the tears that filled her eyes. She hadn't been looking to fall in love. She'd never desired to fall in love. But she had. With Tanner. And until this moment she hadn't realized how desperately she'd wanted to be seated in the truck next to him when he returned to Foxrun.

She wept with grief over what might have been,

then wept because for the first time she wondered if she really could be enough for the baby she might possibly be carrying.

It took over fifteen minutes for Tanner to retrieve his truck from the parking garage where he had parked it when he'd first arrived into town.

As he waited for the attendant to retrieve it, he leaned against the office building. The air smelled of tires, oil and exhaust, but his thoughts were strictly on the woman he'd just walked away from.

Damn her for twisting his certainties into doubts, for making him question answers he'd believed he'd possessed. He scuffed a boot against the asphalt, wondering why her parting words had pierced through him like arrows of truth.

Had he been hanging on to Gina because he'd been afraid to face the emptiness of his life without her? Had it been fear for her that had driven him to come to Kansas City to bring her home or had it been fear for himself?

He had to admit there was a part of him that was proud of Gina for sticking to her guns and refusing to allow him to drag her where she didn't want to go.

He was proud of how she had handled the attempted purse snatching. She'd done everything right. She'd had her purse looped around her neck where it couldn't easily be plucked away from her. She'd screamed loudly for help, then she'd gone immediately to the police. She'd handled the entire incident extremely well.

A squeal of tires indicated the imminent arrival of his truck. Within minutes he'd paid the attendant and pulled out of the downtown parking garage.

Immediately he turned on the radio, hoping to drown out his thoughts. However, even Garth Brooks and his friends in low places couldn't keep her out of his head.

Colette. Her name resounded inside him. The memory of her in his arms tormented him. The sound of her laughter rang in his heart.

He couldn't believe the lengths she'd gone to in order to create a family for herself. Artificial insemination. How could she have even considered such a thing? Artificial insemination was fine for women who were married and had found the normal route of getting pregnant impossible. But Tanner had never understood why single women would make a conscious choice to parent alone.

It's none of my business, he told himself firmly. She was none of his business. She was stubborn and fiercely independent and didn't recognize the neediness inside herself.

Just like you, a small voice replied. "Shut up," he muttered irritably to the tiny voice. He turned up the radio, took the entrance ramp for the interstate and headed west, home to Two Hearts.

* * *

Colette stood in her bathroom and pulled the pregnancy test out of the plastic shopping bag. Her fingers trembled as she opened the box and pulled out the test instrument and the directions.

She read the directions quickly, then looked at her reflection in the mirror over the sink. Her eyes were slightly swollen from her morning of tears and her pale face radiated the torment of heartbreak that ached inside her.

Tanner. Tanner. His name reverberated inside the chambers of her heart bringing with it an echo of pain each time it chimed inside her.

Why, why had he come into her life and given her a glimpse of what it would be like to be loved by him forever? Why had he shown her all the things she'd miss if she continued to choose a life alone?

She shook her head. She couldn't think about that, she thought as she scanned the directions to the test one last time. She absolutely, positively couldn't think about him.

Four weeks ago the only wish in her life had been to be pregnant, and she'd opted to become a single parent. At that time she'd been so certain that she was doing the right thing. Now she wasn't so sure.

The things that Tanner had said to her had struck a chord deep inside her. Was she expecting a baby to fill the emptiness that her relationship with her mother had created inside her? If so, it was a huge bit of baggage to place on a baby.

Darn Tanner Rothman, anyway, she thought angrily. She'd been perfectly happy with her life before he came along. And now that life seemed so achingly empty.

Four weeks ago all she'd wanted was to be pregnant and run her shop, but that had been before she'd met him, before she'd fallen in love with him and had her heart broken into a million little pieces.

She stared down at the directions one last time. She'd bought the test she'd thought would be easiest to read. Within three minutes either a plus or minus sign would appear in the test window. Plus meant pregnant. Minus meant not pregnant.

Simple. Easy. Except that since she'd met Tanner, her life had suddenly become complicated and she wasn't sure anymore exactly what she wanted.

Deciding she could put it off no longer, she took the test, then set it on the counter and prepared to wait the three minutes.

Only seconds had passed when the doorbell rang. Probably Gina, Colette thought. She often forgot her key. With a quick glance of the test stick, which showed nothing, Colette left her bathroom, went through her bedroom and opened the front door.

"Tanner!" she gasped in surprise.

"We need to talk," he said, and walked into the apartment without invitation. He sat on the sofa and gazed at her expectantly.

"I think we've said all we need to say to each

other,'' she replied, fighting to inject coolness into her tone.

"Maybe you did, but I didn't say everything I need to say to you. Come here.'' He patted the sofa next to him.

She didn't want to sit next to him. She desperately wanted to sit next to him. She closed the door, then folded her arms over her chest and remained where she stood.

"If you intend to lecture me about my life, then you can just get right off my sofa and head back out of town," she said.

She unfolded her arms and began to pace in front of where he sat, unable to stand still. "I know you're a traditional man and you disapprove of everything about me, but that doesn't mean you have a right to tell me how much you disapprove of me and my life-style.''

"I didn't come back here to tell you that.'' He leaned forward and raked a hand through his hair. "You were right, you know.''

She stopped pacing and looked at him in surprise. "Right about what?''

"About me not wanting to let go of Gina despite the fact that it's time to do just that. You were right when you said I'd raised her to be strong and inde-pendent and now it's time to step back and let her be." He stood. "Of course, that doesn't mean I'm not going to worry about her and I'm not going to continue to be a large part of her life."

"I'm glad, Tanner, but you didn't have to come back here just to tell me that." Looking at him again just renewed the pain in her heart. Why was he here? Had he truly no idea how just seeing him again tormented her?

"Dammit, Colette," he said suddenly, surprising her. He swiped a hand through his hair once again then took several steps toward her. "I didn't come back here to talk about Gina. I was all set to head back home and get on with my life."

"So why didn't you?" She fought against the tears that once again threatened, tears she'd thought she'd depleted where he was concerned.

"I couldn't," he exclaimed, a touch of anger in his voice. "I tried. I cranked up the radio and hit the interstate heading west, but I couldn't get you out of my head."

Again she looked at him in surprise. "What are you talking about?" she asked, disturbed by the soft vulnerability in her own voice.

"I'm talking about the fact that somehow, some way, you've managed to crawl inside me." His eyes were the deepest blue she'd ever seen them. "When I take a breath, I think of your scent. I hear your laughter in my ears, feel your skin beneath my fingertips."

She sat in one of the chairs, unsure her legs would

hold her any longer as she heard the words fall from his lips.

He walked over and stood directly in front of her chair, his gorgeous eyes deep blue and intense. "I don't know how this happened," he said, his tone filled with frustration. "This was supposed to be a simple trip to the city to get Gina to come home, but from the moment I first laid eyes on you, nothing has been simple."

A sweet warmth fluttered through her as she realized that apparently Gina had been wrong. Tanner hadn't just kissed her to get her on his side. He hadn't held her in his arms just to manipulate her.

"As crazy as it sounds, in the past two weeks I've managed to fall head over heels in love with you. And to be honest with you, the whole thing really makes me mad." He glared at her, as if his emotional turmoil was all her fault.

He loved her. Joy filled her up, but it was a joy tempered with a dose of heartbreaking reality. "Mad?" she asked. "Why?"

"Because you live here and have a business to run. You've made it clear that you believe you don't need me, that you don't need anyone." His voice broke, and in the depths of his eyes she saw a heartbreak to rival her own.

He shoved his hands in his pockets and continued to hold her gaze. "I don't even know how you feel about me, but the one thing I do know is that there is no point in me asking you to marry me or in me asking you to share my life at Two Hearts.''

It had hurt when he'd left earlier and she'd believed he'd used her. But the love that shone so fully from his eyes now felt like a killing pain deep inside her.

There was a part of her that desperately wanted to reach for the love, for the future he held out to her, and there was a part of her that was desperately afraid.

The conflicting emotions drew tears to her eyes as her joy was tempered with despair. How could she give up all she'd accomplished here in exchange for love? Wouldn't that make her just like her mother? Her tears came faster.

''Colette?'' Tanner knelt down beside where she sat and took one of her hands in his. ''Why are you crying?''

She squeezed her eyes tightly shut, unwilling to look at him, unwilling to see all that she was giving up shining from his eyes. ''I'm crying because I love you, too.'' She finally managed to say in a whisper. ''And because it frightens me how much I want to be your wife and live at Two Hearts.''

She gasped, and her eyes snapped open as he pulled her up from the chair and into his arms. ''Tell me what you're afraid of, Colette.''

How could she explain to him that she was terrified that she'd lose herself in him, that her own identity would vanish.

He took his thumbs and gently swiped at her tears.

"Colette, I love you and you say you love me, so what is making you so unhappy?"

She stepped out of his embrace. "Don't you see, it's all so impossible. If I agree to marry you, if I go with you to Foxrun and forget my life here, then I'm just like my mother, giving up everything I am for a man."

"Colette." He captured her in his arms once again. "You are one of the strongest and most independent women I have ever known. There is no way in this world you could ever be like your mother. I wouldn't be in love with you if you were weak."

He stepped back from her, frustration etched across his forehead. "And I would never ask you to give up what you have built here. We'll figure something out." His eyes loved her. "I won't live my life without you."

In those simple, wonderful words, Colette's fears gave way and her heart opened with a love so intense it filled her up. And in that love there was no room for fear. "Ask me, Tanner. Ask me to marry you. Ask me to make Foxrun and Two Hearts my home." Her voice trembled with emotion.

Almost before the words were out of her mouth he took her hands in his. "Marry me, Colette. Share my life at Two Hearts and build a family with me. Marry me and make me the happiest man on earth."

"Yes," she said. "Yes, I want that." Tears once

again filled her eyes as he pulled her against him and captured her lips with his.

His kiss promised heated passion and sweet, abiding love, and in that kiss, in that love that flowed from him, she knew the decision she had made was the right one.

When the kiss ended, he led her to the sofa and they sat down side by side, her hands held tight by his. His gaze held hers searchingly. "Colette, I know how hard you've worked to make your baby boutique successful."

She heard the questions in his voice, knew he was worried about how she would handle giving up the boutique. She smiled at him, sure of herself, her decisions and the path she was about to take.

"You know, Tanner, I've got this terrific, bright, responsible woman working for me, and I think with a month or two of training she could run the store here just fine."

"You really think she could handle it?"

"Without doubt." His hand squeezed hers and she continued, "And you said that all the women in Foxrun are looking to get married and that means they're going to have babies. I think Foxrun would be a good place to open up a little branch of the Little Bit Baby Boutique."

He opened his mouth to say something, but she shook her head, indicating she wasn't finished yet. "I know you probably figured you'd marry a traditional kind of woman who wouldn't work outside the home, but, Tanner, I..."

"Shhh." He stopped her by leaning forward and kissing her gently. "I love you, Colette, and I'll support you in everything you want to do. All I want is to make you happy for the rest of your life."

Colette had never known such happiness. She was filled up with it, awed by the wellspring of happiness that bubbled inside her. But as she suddenly remembered the pregnancy test, her joy dimmed.

He hadn't mentioned her artificial insemination, and she wondered if perhaps he'd forgotten about it. She pulled her hands from his. "Tanner, have you forgotten that it's possible I might be pregnant?" She held her breath, wondering if all would be lost after all.

His gaze was gentle and the expression of love on his face didn't waver. "No, I haven't forgotten. I keep thinking if you try to raise that baby alone, then who is he going to buy ugly ties for on Father's Day? Who's going to teach him to fish? That baby is part of you and I love you and..."

Whatever else he was about to say was lost as Colette threw herself into his arms and kissed him with all the passion and love she had inside her.

"I took a pregnancy test right before you came back here," she said when the kiss ended.

"And what was the result?" he asked.

"I don't know. You got here and I haven't checked the results."

He smiled indulgently. "Then I guess we'd better go check."

Together they got up off the sofa and headed into Colette's bathroom. Colette's heartbeat pounded loudly in her ears. For the first time she wasn't sure what she hoped to find when she viewed the results. Where before she'd wanted a baby, now she wanted Tanner's baby.

She was just about to step into the bathroom when Tanner took her hand and drew her into his arms. "I just want to tell you one thing before you look."

"What?"

He ran a finger down her cheek and for a moment she felt as if she could drown in the love that flowed from his eyes. "If you're pregnant, then I'm going to love that baby with all my heart and soul. And if you aren't pregnant, then that's the first thing we'll work on the moment we say our vows."

Sweet heat flooded through her as she thought of making love to him. "You promise?"

He grinned, that slow sexy smile of his. "Oh, yes, I promise. In fact, as far as I'm concerned we don't have to wait a minute for me to start making good on that promise."

Again warmth swept through her as she saw the flames of desire and the burning embers of love in his eyes. She squeezed his hand once, then went into the bathroom and looked at the test.

Plus sign she was pregnant...minus sign she was not. A minus sign winked at her from the test window. She stepped out to where Tanner waited. "I'm not pregnant," she said.

"Oh, darlin', are you terribly disappointed?"

She smiled and moved back into his embrace. "Disappointed? How can I be disappointed that the first baby I'll have will be that of the man I love?"

"I love you, Colette," he whispered into her ear, then kissed her again in a kiss that promised the kind of future Colette had never believed possible for herself.

Epilogue

Colette stood and looked at herself in the floor-length mirror in the back room of the Foxrun Community Center. Outside the room, in the main hall, it seemed that most of the town had turned out for her wedding to Tanner.

It had been just a little more than six weeks since she and Tanner had confessed their love for each other. It had been the busiest six weeks of Colette's life. Not only had she trained Gina in every aspect of the business, but she'd also visited the ranch and rented a building in Foxrun that would be the new site of a Little Bit Baby Boutique.

It had been a magical time, and each day her love for Tanner had deepened. And within minutes she would become his wife. A shiver of delight raced through her.

She turned as the door opened, and smiled as Gina flew in, resplendent in a long pink dress that accentuated her lovely dark hair.

"Oh, Colette!" She clapped her hands together as she hurried to where Colette stood. "You look positively beautiful. I'm so glad you opted for a traditional wedding gown."

Colette turned away from the mirror and grinned. "Your brother insisted. He said since I was only getting married once in my life, I should go all out and do it right. And you know how your brother is..."

"Cursedly stubborn," they both chorused together, then laughed.

"I'm sorry your mother won't be here," Gina said when their laughter had died.

The pain that thoughts of her mother had always brought had lessened, and now a stab of pity shot through her. "It's her loss," Colette replied. "She'll never be happy and I can't change that. Besides, I have all the family I need right here, and a home and a town that I've positively fallen in love with."

Gina reached out and hugged Colette. "I'm so happy for you, Colette. And I've never seen Tanner so happy. I just know you're going to have a wonderful life together."

They both turned as a knock sounded on the door. "Come in," Colette called.

Bailey Jenkins, the town veterinarian and a good

friend of Tanner's, stuck his head inside. "Everyone is ready. We're just waiting for the bride."

"We'll be right out," Gina replied. She looked back at Colette. "Are you ready?"

Colette drew a deep breath and nodded. Together the two women stepped out of the back room and walked down a corridor to the main hall. A white walkway strewn with rose petals awaited her, and at the end of the walk stood Tanner.

As the bridal march began and Gina and Bailey walked down the aisle toward the minister, Colette had eyes only for the man who was about to become her husband.

He looked achingly handsome in a white tuxedo and tails, and the smile that curved his lips made her heart sing with joy.

She started down the aisle slowly, her gaze locked with Tanner's. As she reached the midway point she quickened her pace, half running toward the handsome, loving, "cursedly stubborn" cowboy who had opened the world of love.

* * * * *

Don't miss the other half of Carla's
THE PREGNANCY TEST *duo*

IF THE STICK TURNS PINK...

*also available this month from
Silhouette Romance.*

COMING NEXT MONTH